SUBURBAN WATCHDOGS

KARMA IS A... FEMALE DOG

BURDEN OF PROOFREADING

Publishing

A COMEDY BY

TIFFANY ANDREA

ISBN: 978-1-990724-00-8

Cover Design by: Burden of Proofreading Publishing featuring photos by Molikaan via CanStockPhoto

Interior Graphics by Pillerss

For my husband, Ryan.

For years, the kids and I have suffered through your endless terrible dad jokes. Thank you for providing the inspiration for this story.

Despite the bad jokes, which I'll tolerate because I love to hear you laugh, you've been everything I could have asked for in a husband and father. Our family will forever be my greatest accomplishment, and you, my greatest love.

However, you better read this one, or you're sleeping on the couch.

Happy Anniversary. I love you.

TABLE OF CONTENTS

UNLAWFUL ASSEMBLY

The situation may not have started out personal, but it became more personal than underwear the moment Alliston's most notorious criminals rolled into the west side of town looking for a fight. If that's what they wanted, that's what they'd get. At least, in theory. Maybe not a *fight* fight, but some harsh words or an intimidating scowl. Yeah, that'd do the trick.

"We need something sticky!" Morrie whispered.

"I'm on it." Justin darted down the dark alley between the doctor's office and the daycare. A moment later, he handed Morrie a branch. "Here, I got one."

Morrie stared at Justin with narrowed eyebrows, feeling the length of the branch for sap, or something that would help him adhere the new tracking device to the vehicle they wanted to follow. The built-in magnet was not doing its job. "Why did you bring this?"

"You said you needed something sticky."

"This isn't sticky."

"That's where you're wrong." He winked. "That there is the perfect stick."

Morrie felt like he'd bitten off more than he could chew with his motley crew of neighbours. They quickly evolved from a group of dads watching sports and movies in Joshua Miller's basement into a vigilante gang seeking justice for their town's recent spike in crime and trying to keep their families safe. With burglaries on the rise and police unable to prevent them, the four fathers took matters into their own hands.

Armed with bear mace and Canadian Tire's best walkie-talkies, the group of blue-collar suburbanites looked for restitution for the trouble the assailants had caused. After weeks of surveillance and close calls, they tracked the criminals down to a local doctor's office.

"No movement at the rear," Garcia relayed through the handheld radio.

"Ten-four," Justin responded. "Let's wait at the front. We'll have them surrounded."

"Hold on a second. I've got something in my shoe." Morrie crouched down, but not before scanning his surroundings for potential dangers.

"I'm pretty sure it's your foot."

Morrie suppressed a groan as he pulled a pebble from his sneaker. "Maybe we should call the police now."

"No way, man. This is our takedown. We've worked for months to stop these guys."

The two men crouched beside the stairs leading out of the building, concealing themselves behind spruce hedge.

"I don't know. What if they have guns or something? I will not die over some random after-hours burglary when no one else is in danger." The pool of nerves in Morrie's stomach was making decisions on his behalf; he sensed something was going to go terribly wrong.

"Don't be a pansy. We've got bear mace, so we'll be fine. We could literally take down a bear." Justin's intense expression seemed to convey more than his words did, so Morrie didn't argue.

What could go wrong? As the brains of the operation, and at times, the only one with *any* brains, Wesley Morris felt obligated to stay and look after his group of friends. He also knew that the responsible thing to do would be to call the police. He pulled his phone from his back pocket to dial 911.

Before Morrie could press send, an alarm started wailing, and without having time to comprehend what was happening, the front door of the doctor's office flew open. Three men came running out, each carrying a duffel bag of whatever goods they had been seeking.

Without thinking through the potential consequences, as per usual, Justin took the branch he had earlier retrieved and thrusted it through the railing toward the tall man in the front of the group, causing him to trip. The two men trailing behind were too close to avoid a collision, so within a split second, the three of them lay in a tangled mess on the concrete stairs outside of the doctor's office.

Justin winked at Morrie again. "See, that was the perfect stick."

Morrie rolled his eyes, but when they landed back on the group of men in front of them, all three were standing, pointing guns at the interfering fathers.

"Who the hell are you?" the gruff voice of the tall man asked, staring down at them from behind the grip of his handgun.

"We're nobody," Morrie replied. His nerves were back with a vengeance, causing his voice to shake.

"We're not nobody. We're the Suburban Watchdogs, and we want you to stop terrorizing our town."

"Suburban Watchdogs?" the tall man replied as he huffed a mocking laugh.

"That's right." Justin puffed out his chest to make his five-foot-five, one-hundred-thirty-pound frame more intimidating. "And we don't like what y'all have been doing. So why don't you just pack up and leave town?"

"It doesn't appear you have the upper hand here, Watchdog. I reckon we'll keep doing whatever it is we want because dead men don't have opinions."

Justin still failed to grasp the severity of the situation. "You don't know who you're up against, Beanstalk."

"They have guns. Shut up," Morrie begged.

"Stop being a wuss." Justin turned to the obscenely tall man. "What are you? A stay-at-home astronaut?"

The greying ginger man-mountain scowled as his face turned a deeper shade of red. Obviously, he had a hot temper and Justin's moronic banter was throwing gasoline into the inferno. "What are you? A jockey? I could keep you in my pocket."

"Do you drive around with your head out of the sunroof?" Justin inched closer to the man, but they still remained ten feet apart.

Morrie tucked himself in behind his friend. He was not about to die a hero for a friend who wanted to engage in a battle of wits with no ammunition.

"What do you drive? A minivan?" The tall man stepped closer to Justin and Morrie, looking angrier by the second.

"Yeah, actually I do!" Justin reduced the distance between them again, undeterred by the confrontation. "A blue one!"

Morrie thought, *at least they're evenly matched*.

"Are you always this stupid or is today a special occasion?" the chubby burglar with unkempt hair asked, leaning his head around his taller cohort.

"How did you get here? Did someone leave your cage open?" Justin replied.

Morrie felt more nervous each time his friend opened his mouth. Justin offered as much protection from a bullet as a sheet of drywall, and Morrie didn't feel right about using the small man as a shield, anyway. He'd never been a coward before, but he was clueless as to how they'd get out of the mess they were in.

Just when Morrie was convinced they were going to die, and he'd never see his beautiful wife, Nicole, or his two children again, Justin uttered something even more surprising.

"Chock-a-block!"

The next thing Morrie heard was a gunshot.

KIDNAPPING

FIVE MONTHS EARLIER

Joshua Miller, known by his friends as Josh, married his wife, Lily, fourteen years ago. They were high school sweethearts and wed once Lily finished college at age twenty-one. Josh forewent college because academics were never his strong suit, and he decided to pay for his younger brother's post-secondary education since their mother was unable to afford it. He took a job in construction after leaving high school, and though it was backbreaking and laborious, it was well within his skill set and he enjoyed it. He was able to put his brother through school and eventually, he and Lily bought their home in Alliston—a mid-sized farming town in Ontario.

It was at their new home where they connected with other young families like themselves. Their daughters, Daisy and Dahlia, who were ten and eight, were happy young girls involved in many extra-curricular activities. They attended an elementary school down the road with the other neighbourhood kids, which meant the parents had bonded over the endless number of fundraisers and spirit days. They were fortunate enough to find a "village" to raise their children.

Lily, who had always been a supportive wife, encouraged Josh to convert the basement of their home into a "man cave," so he'd have a space to unwind after a long day at work. There were more Barbie cars and doll clothes than jerseys and dart boards, but at least he had the eighty-inch TV for movie or hockey game nights with the guys.

Josh's three neighbourhood friends, Justin Peterson, Brendon Garcia, and Wesley Morris, were coming over to watch a movie since there were no exciting sports on for their weekly guys' night. They agreed to watch an old mafia movie they were all big fans of. None of them had seen it for years, so it would still be interesting, but if they talked through it, everyone would still know what was going on—well, maybe not Justin—he didn't know much.

Josh stood in the basement when he heard the doorbell ring, then his wife's footsteps as she headed to welcome his guests. Within a moment, his three friends were standing in the basement with him, and he offered them each a drink. None of them were heavy drinkers, but they liked to partake a little during their Friday night gatherings.

After everyone greeted Josh and settled in, Justin started complaining about his wife, Scarlett. Together, they had a nine-year-old son, Oliver, and that was all they had in common. "I swear, guys, my wife is like a newspaper. New issue every day. Only difference is, I can't toss them in the recycling and be done with it."

"Why don't you divorce her?" Brendon asked.

"I don't know. I can't bring myself to call it quits for real. Ollie would be caught in the middle, and it gets messy." Justin took a sip of his beer, appearing deep in thought, which was unlikely.

"Yeah, I get it. It's expensive too."

The three other men looked at Brendon, not surprised his take on the matter would come down to the cost. He was a notorious cheapskate.

After another fifteen minutes of repeating his wife's complaints, Justin implored, "Let's forget about the drama and get to the movie. There's no problem some good old-fashioned mobsters can't solve."

The men remained silent for the first thirty minutes of the movie before Justin spoke up again. "Ollie said there was a kid napping at school the other day."

"What? How did I not hear about it?" Morrie asked with wide eyes after choking back the drink he nearly spit out.

"It was no big deal. The teacher woke him up, and he got detention, but I guess everyone was teasing him," Justin replied with a shoulder shrug.

Morrie heaved out a sigh. Kid *napping*, not a kidnapping. "Justin, you're about as sharp as a bowling ball. Do you think before you speak?"

"That doesn't make any sense." Justin shook his head. "Bowling balls aren't even sharp."

"Exactly." Morrie rolled his eyes—a frequent occurrence.

"Did you hear *The Gadget Factory* was robbed a few nights ago?" Brendon asked.

Morrie hesitated before clarifying, "As in burglarized, or a man named Rob walked in? With you guys, I can never tell."

"No, three guys broke in sometime in the evening, tied up two employees, and stole whatever they could get their hands on. The news report didn't say too much, but they made off with a lot, apparently," Brendon explained. "Who would have thought? In our little town?"

"No kidding? I'll have to look up the story. I haven't heard anything." Morrie drifted off into thought, concerned about a serious crime so close to home. The electronics store in question was less than a mile from their home in the opposite direction from the kids' school.

"I didn't hear anything about it either, but I heard sirens the other night. Makes sense if that's what it was about." Josh noted, since sirens in their area were uncommon. "Did they catch the guys?"

"Not last I heard. They're still on the loose." Brendon was unfazed by the potential danger as he never broke his focus on the massive TV. "They just said there were three men. One was very tall."

"I don't like the idea of some criminals running around our little town. I wish I could go all 'Fat Tony' on them." Justin pushed out his non-existent gut.

"Who's Fat Tony?" Josh asked with a raised eyebrow.

"That's my gangster name. You know? Fat Tony." Justin's pupils threatened to escape the corners of his eyes as he glared at his friends from the left end of the sofa.

"Justin, you're not even a little fat," Brendon pointed out. He eyed his own dad bod he'd been perfecting for the better part of a decade, making him more qualified to be Fat Tony.

"That's the beauty of it. It's ironic. I'm a skinny, blond guy. Nobody would catch on that I was Fat Tony." Justin shoved some salt and vinegar chips in his mouth.

"Right." Morrie shook his head and stared at his friend for a moment, wondering how he found his way out of the womb. He probably needed a c-section because he got lost on his way to the birth canal.

"Morrie here can be 'Whitey', and Josh, you can be 'Corky'," Justin continued.

11

"Corky? Why would you call me Corky? And Morrie is Jamaican! We need better names than those. Like... I don't know. But something else."

"No. Ya see? It's the perfect way to throw everyone off your trail. Irony." Justin tapped his temple with his index finger. "Whitey is a great gangster name, like Whitey Bulger."

"I'm pretty sure he was called whitey because of his hair. The name doesn't really suit me, Justin."

"Fat Tony." Justin levelled Morrie with a glare. As nonsensical as the man could be, he was dead serious at that moment. "That's why it's ironic. Because it *doesn't* fit you at all."

"So why Corky?" The smile lines around Josh's mouth and eyes deepened.

"Corky. From *Corky Romano*. He protects his family by playing both sides of the law."

Wires were getting crossed and Josh's face expressed the same level of confusion as the other men who were listening to Justin come up with gangster names. "I don't think that's ironic in this situation."

"No, but it's my favourite gangster movie." Justin shrugged.

Josh and Morrie locked eyes with each other, exchanging their opinions without a word. Josh mouthed, 'Corky?'

Morrie chuckled and returned, 'Whitey?'

After a long tilt of his beer, Justin added, "Brendon can be 'Scarface', but we'll call him 'Scar'."

"But I do have a scar." Brendon pointed to his lower lip that was split in a skiing accident—an accident where he kicked himself in the lip with his ski.

Justin stared at Brendon, inspecting his minuscule scar. "Not a cool one. It's still ironic."

"Okay, so if we all have gangster names, what do we call our gang?" Josh asked with a glint of amusement in his eyes.

"Turf Posse. No, wait, Ghetto Gang." Justin spewed off random names in between mouthfuls of chips.

"Fat Tony, we don't live in the ghetto." Morrie grumbled, tired of inspecting the back of his own head from all the eye-rolling he had been doing.

"Fine. What about The Block Band? No, I've got it. Suburban Watchdogs," Justin declared.

"Yeah, Suburban Watchdogs," agreed Josh. "I like it. Sounds like a cooler version of Neighbourhood Watch."

"Fat Tony, Whitey, Corky, and Scar of the Suburban Watchdogs. Sounds like a rag-tag group of culturally confused misfits." Morrie chuckled, picturing the mayhem that would come from assembling his friends to accomplish anything beyond beer drinking and arguing over sports. They couldn't even arrange a bake sale.

"I don't know what that means," Justin replied, "but we'll need uniforms."

The other three men stared at Justin, unsure if he was serious. They had repeatedly overestimated the number of functioning brain cells he possessed, so one could never be sure.

"Uniforms?" Brendon asked, scrunching his nose.

"Yeah. Nothing obvious," Justin replied. "We can't be walking around in tailored suits; that would be too... what's the word?"

Morrie waited for whatever stupid thing was about to come out of his neighbour's mouth, but after a few seconds of watching the wheels spin in Justin's head, he prompted him with some suggestions. "Suspicious? Uncomfortable?"

"No, expensive. Anyway, we need to find something so people take us seriously. Leave it to me. I'll find the perfect solution." Justin's words never inspired much confidence. It really was a miracle when he got his trash to the curb on the right day.

Brendon cringed. "Let's just pick something we all have already. I don't want to spend money on something stupid."

"You are the cheapest person I've ever met." Morrie was always surprised by the extreme lengths Brendon would go to in order to save a dollar. There's frugal, there's cheap, and there's Brendon.

"Nah, I don't buy it," Brendon replied. "Have you ever seen that cheapskate show on TV? Some guys pick anniversary gifts out of dumpsters." He took a sip of beer, chasing it with a few chips, but squinting his eyes from the burn of the vinegar flavour. "They're geniuses."

"You want to give your wife a gift from a dumpster?" Morrie took a second to remind himself to stop being surprised by the nonsense he heard on Friday nights.

"No, I don't have a death wish. I'd just rather buy something practical—like a dishwasher or an oil change. I don't want to waste money on flowers and jewellery." Brendon pointed at the TV, indicating the mafia member's wives decked out in diamonds and furs.

Morrie shook his head. He thought about how lucky Brendon was for having a wife like Anna who put up with him. The woman gave him three beautiful children, and as far as Morrie could tell, she was a great wife and mother, all while working as an office administrator for a local diagnostics clinic. "Buddy, you know most people live and learn—you just live. Don't you remember a couple of years back when you bought Anna the vacuum?"

Brendon leaned forward from his spot on the couch. "Hey, that was a Dyson! She should have been more appreciative!"

"I agree, man. Those things ain't cheap." Justin patted his friend on the shoulder to placate him. Of course, Justin would agree.

"You're telling me. I had to save up my loyalty rewards for years to buy that for her. Then she had the nerve to hit me with the attachment. Now it just collects dust."

Morrie couldn't blame Anna for her reaction. "Women like romance sometimes. She deserves something to make her feel special."

"Heck, I was trying. She's always complaining about the mess left around. I thought it would help."

15

Nope. Morrie decided it was not even worth continuing that conversation. It's one thing if your wife asked for a vacuum, or you purchased it together, but buying one for an anniversary as an attempted romantic gesture was a bit presumptuous—and evidently dangerous. This was more evidence that these men were too different to team up for anything.

The men fell into another comfortable silence as they continued watching their movie. The incessant munching, gulping, and burping sounded like a symphony of bad manners, but they all focused on the cinematic masterpiece that depicted life in the American Mafia. It looked easy enough.

After the credits rolled and the men consumed every crumb of sustenance, they continued joking around about their newly formed "gang." Well, three out of four of them viewed it as a joke. Justin appeared ready to go "Fat Tony" on anyone attempting to jaywalk. For some reason, he was really amped up by the idea.

After midnight, Josh saw his friends out since his wife and daughters were already in bed. The entire neighbourhood was dark and quiet. "All right guys, I'll see you around."

"G'night Watchdogs!" Justin pointed finger guns at everyone and acted like he was trying to win the Wild West.

Morrie again rolled his eyes. "Justin, I swear when I look into your eyes, I can see straight to the back of your skull."

"Whitey, you make no sense, man."

"Point proven. And stop calling me Whitey. Morrie, Wesley, even Wes is fine, but I'm no Whitey."

"Irony, brother." Justin tapped his head again as he winked at Morrie.

Morrie released an exasperated sigh. "Goodnight, guys. I'll see you around."

Everyone said their goodbyes and headed to their own homes for the night. Little did they know the very men who had terrorized their town just a few days prior would be back at it again very soon.

IDENTITY THEFT

Gordon Wright spent his childhood with a single mom who insisted if he worked hard enough, he could be anyone he wanted. Unfortunately for Gordon, identity theft was a crime, and he had the rap sheet to prove it. His mom failed to make her point obvious, but since she passed when Gordon was a teenager, he was unable to seek further clarification.

Finding well-paying work when you've got a criminal record was hard. Beyond that, Gord wasn't cut out for life as a line cook or pre-school teacher. He stood over seven feet tall, 260lbs, and if he stripped down, he could blend in a snowbank. Outdoor work wasn't ideal because he hadn't inherited enough melanin to handle it, and he never worked well with others. The copper-coloured hair of his childhood would tell you he had a fiery temper, and the two other men on his heist crew would agree. Gord's hair may have faded thanks to the overwhelming grey, but his temper had not.

"We're almost done offloading the electronics, then we'll have enough petty cash to buy a new van. I'll go back to Rodney and get one with a stripped VIN." Nelson Dunne, Gordon's third crew member, was the fence who sold all of their stolen goods. Gordon paid him well for his trouble, and even though he was irritating when he gave attitude, he was excellent at his job.

"Dunne, make sure you get one with three seats this time. I'm tired of bouncing around in the back." Earle Cady was a different story. He and Gord had been friends since they were kids and after they got into some trouble a while back that landed Earle with a criminal record longer than Gord's, work wasn't easy for him to find either. Not once did he rat on Gord, though, so for that, the big man was grateful. That's criminal conduct 101. Earle's loyalty earned him a permanent spot alongside Gord.

"Yeah, yeah. Quit your whining. It's not easy finding vehicles this behemoth can fit in, so we take what we can get."

Earle sniggered, looking at his giant friend.

"Ha, ha. More jokes about the big guy." Gord folded up the newspaper he had been browsing and tossed it into the nearby trash can. Refusing to recycle was just one more act of rebellion on his part. "Do you think—"

"Yeah, all the time." Earle stared back at him with a stupid grin on his face.

"That's not what I was asking. Do you think—"

"Yep." Earle's face made it obvious he loved the reaction he got from irritating the big man. His temper was unpredictable, but Earle measured more than eighteen inches shorter and although they weighed the same, he was a lot more agile.

"Stop that. I'm trying to ask something." Gord levelled Earle with a scowl, but it was not as effective as it was on others. He and Earle had been friends for too long. Earle knew every weakness.

"Ask away."

"Thank you." Gord sucked in a deep breath to compose himself, but there was practically steam coming from his ears.

"You're welcome."

"Do you think... ugh, now I forgot what I was going to ask." Each year older Gord got, he noticed his memory faltering more and more, but no one could frazzle him as effectively as Earle.

"Do you think?" Earle smirked and raised his eyebrows, waiting for a reaction.

Gord growled, swiping his big arm out to connect with Earle's chin, but missed. Earle was too quick, and after decades as friends, he knew how to predict Gord's boiling point.

Earle scampered off, laughing, which only irritated Gord more. If they weren't so good at what they did as a team, he'd pound that little man into the ground. No one else got away with making a fool of him.

"I remember now," Gord told Nelson. "Do you think we can get a van with no logos or anything on the side? It's easy enough to cover the plates, but this one"—he hooked a thumb, gesturing toward the driveway—"has that stupid beaver on the side. If we're caught on camera in something obvious, that makes it harder to hide in plain sight."

"Sure thing, boss," Nelson dutifully replied.

Their business model was simple. Keep 'em guessing. The crew moved from one town to another, working in a new location for a few months before relocating. They never kept a vehicle for more than a month. They wouldn't hit the same type of mark twice in a row. Their customer base was varied and expendable, so they could move from one place to another without missing anyone. There were always people willing to buy illicit goods, no matter where you went; you just needed to know where to look. Crime was the one industry you could find anywhere in the world.

Their most recent place was, by far, the smallest town they'd ever hit. They found a house to rent in the middle of farm country, which allowed them privacy when they came and went at unusual hours. The property owners only cared if the rent was paid on time, and otherwise didn't bother them. It was a perfect location to set up their criminal enterprise for a few months. Especially because it was only an hour from the city, and small-town businesses had less security. They were sorely mistaken, thinking they were impervious to criminal activity.

Gord and his crew were planning to dish out some hard lessons.

From his spot at the kitchen table, Gord counted their latest bounty from the electronics store robbery, comparing it to the spreadsheet on his laptop. He may be a criminal, but he was an organized one. Keeping a tally of expenses leading up to the job, what was taken, and the profit turned on each item allowed him to tune their enterprise as they went, so they no longer wasted time on jobs that didn't pay. Wasting time and money was one of Gord's biggest pet peeves.

If everything went to plan, they'd make enough from their next five jobs to cover all expenses for the duration of their stay in the paltry little farming town and top up their retirement fund with a good chunk of cash.

The plans laid out in front of them detailed the targets they intended to hit between February and June before they'd sail off into the sunset. Literally.

Over the past six years, the three men worked together without being caught—without even the slightest interference. They stored up a decent nest egg of over six million dollars between them, and once they were done with the last of their planned jobs, it would be time to retire. Gord and Earle were both nearing fifty and not as spry as they once were. Nelson was the young cat, only forty-one, but he was more than ready to call it quits and move to a tropical island somewhere.

Everything was going perfectly to plan.

This place was an easy mark. Basic alarm system, security cameras run on Wi-Fi—a rookie mistake as far as legitimate security goes, but a popular option—and plenty of petty cash on hand.

Beyond planning heists, Gord was an expert in cracking safes. He was an apprentice of sorts, working with a gentleman who knew all the old-school methods to get into analog safes with dials or keys, but being a student of criminal life, Gord expanded his skill set significantly, learning to crack digital safes as well. There had never been one that he couldn't beat—a point of pride for the big man.

Nelson and Earle were raiding the secondary offices of the small-town furniture store, looking for anything of value. They couldn't exactly haul out dishwashers and microwaves, and black-market profit on those was small-time stuff they were not interested in. The hassle far outweighed the payoff. No, they were there for whatever could fit in their bags that they could make off with in a hurry—cash, electronics, credit card numbers and customer information.

When the safe finally made that sweet, welcome sound, beeping to show it had unlocked, Gord swung open the door, and his jaw dropped, spotting the contents. There, inside, was a lonely envelope of cash. He pulled it open, hoping it was a one-inch stack of hundreds at least, but he was disappointed to discover about $1000 in twenties. His temper flared as fast as his nostrils because that was not what all of their recon had told them to expect. Their weeks of surveillance indicated that the manager only did cash deposits at the bank once weekly. That day was supposed to be Friday. They planned their heist for Thursday for that reason alone. There was no way a furniture store only made $1000 cash in a week. They'd been duped.

Grabbing the door of the safe, Gord yanked on it, throwing it to the ground. He upturned the desk in the office, ransacking every now-sideways drawer. Nothing. Absolutely nothing.

The whole job had been a massive waste of time, which was unacceptable. They would have turned a better profit by panhandling at the intersection nearest the Chernobyl Nuclear Plant.

"Argh," Gord screamed from the showroom, where he had moved on to ripping art off the walls and destroying each one by slamming it over his knee. "This was a total"—slam—"waste"—slam—"of time."

He hooked his massive hands under the side of a cream-coloured leather sofa and upturned that next as his partners watched the show unfold. They were smart enough not to intervene in the man's rampage. Gord continued destroying lamps, glass tables, vases, and anything else he could get his hands on. He flicked open his pocketknife and got to work on the upholstery of every item in the showroom. His anger knew no bounds, and he was determined to make the business owners suffer for not making his life as a criminal easier. This job had now cost them money, and that was unacceptable.

"Gordon. We gotta go. Someone must have heard something by now." Earle stood behind an upright refrigerator, using it as a shield. "Let's cut our losses and get out."

Gord came stomping across the destroyed showroom in his size fifteen boots. "Cut our losses? Do you know how much we're in for on this job? The time? The equipment? Thousands, Earle!" A detail Gord is well aware of thanks to his elaborate spreadsheets. "This was supposed to be an easy cash score."

"I know, but we were wrong. We need to get out of here while we still can."

The outrage Gord felt didn't diminish at all, but he listened to his friend, knowing he was right. "Fine. You drive." He tossed the keys at Nelson and stalked toward the back door.

The ride back to their secluded rental was silent. One measly envelope with some cash that would barely cover their gas and food for the next week had Gord fuming. He couldn't stop himself from slamming a fist into the dashboard. That only made his hand hurt, which made him angrier.

This town is going to face the full wrath of Gordon Wright.

DISORDERLY CONDUCT

More than two weeks after movie night with the guys, Justin was driving home from work, exhausted from a long day as a plumber. He was listening to the local news when they reported there had been a second robbery at *GoldenWood Furniture* on the main street several days earlier. Reports didn't tell what was taken but stated over $50,000 in damage had been done. It was unknown if the robbery was related to the latest incident at *The Gadget Factory*, so police were investigating and exploring all avenues.

Justin didn't need confirmation from the police to tell him what he knew in his gut. He was certain it was the same people, and the Suburban Watchdogs were going to do what the police couldn't before the crime spree got out of hand. No, Justin Peterson would not stand idly by and allow his town to be overtaken by criminals.

With his hands clenched around the steering wheel in outrage, Justin considered the best course of action for him and his friends to proceed. Naturally, the Suburban Watchdogs were missing something important. He pulled over at the side of the road and brought up a search on his phone for what he needed. He took a detour on his way home to pick up a critical addition to their gang.

Justin arrived home later than normal after making a lengthy stop. His wife, Scarlett, was waiting by the door to grill him as soon as he showed his face. Much to her surprise, Justin wasn't the first one to greet her. When the door flew open, a large, slobbery beast tackled Scarlett to the ground. She was sprawled on her back, inside the entryway, being licked into oblivion by the unfamiliar creature. Her screams did nothing to deter the monster, who was determined to lick the roof of Scarlett's mouth.

"Karma, come here, girl," Justin called off the dog, and reached a hand out to help his wife up. "Sorry about that. We have to work on her training. She failed as a guard dog, but she's got a lot of potential."

Scarlett looked like she wanted to hurl after having a dog's tongue in her mouth. "We? What are you talking about? You got a dog without even discussing it with me?"

"I just thought with all the robberies happening in town, having a dog wouldn't be the worst thing." He shrugged.

"It's just about the worst thing, Justin. I don't even *like* dogs." The anger in her eyes was unmistakable. Mostly because Justin was familiar with her rage-stares.

Justin looked at his wife, wondering how he could have ever fallen in love with someone who didn't like dogs. Then again, the Scarlett he fell in love with and the woman before him were two different people and he couldn't figure out when or how it had happened.

"Well, Sweet Cheeks, you're just gonna have to learn to live with her, because she's ours now."

Scarlett stomped off while voicing her disgust over having an uncivilized animal in the house. Justin patted Karma on the head, who was sitting patiently beside him, wagging her tail. The automatic connection she had with Justin made him smile. For the first time in years, he felt appreciated by a female.

Oliver came bounding down the stairs; his bright blond hair was bouncing with each step. "Wow, whose dog is that?"

Karma's tail began tapping against Justin's work boot as she saw the young boy approach. A second later, her entire back end was wagging.

28

"She's ours. I just picked her up. Her name's Karma."

"Karma? That's a weird name." Oliver crouched down on the floor beside Karma and welcomed the licks all over his face. He was much more receptive to dog love than his mother was . "That tickles!" Karma pinned Oliver to the ground, sniffing and licking him, her tail never stopping its rapid back and forth.

The sound of Oliver's laughter and seeing how excited he was made Scarlett's anger worth it. There wasn't anything Justin wouldn't do for his son. If Oliver was happy, then Justin would tolerate Scarlett's wrath.

"Can we take her for a walk, Dad?"

"Yeah sure, Buddy. Get your stuff on."

Temperatures were warming, but being March, there would still be plenty of winter weather left. It wasn't unusual for the temperature to fluctuate from deep freeze to spring-like, one day to the next. March weather in Canada was unpredictable. That day, however, seemed like a good time to take Karma to meet the other Suburban Watchdogs, since it was clear and warm-ish, hovering around ten degrees.

Justin pulled out the gold chain collar and black leash from the shopping bag of items he purchased. "Come on, Karma. Let's go introduce you to the guys."

Justin and Oliver proudly marched Karma out the front door and onto the sidewalk that ran along the south side of the street past the cookie cutter houses in varying shades of orange brick. Their first encounter was their elderly neighbour, June. She was a physically active nonagenarian, and while she had slowed down in recent years, she was still a tough old lady.

"G'day, June," Justin greeted on their way past, but even Karma recognized June was not someone to be messed with. She was Merriam-Webster's definition of cantankerous.

The woman eyed the dog suspiciously. "That's some beast you have there."

"She's great, isn't she, Mrs. Garin?" Oliver was polite to the elderly woman, but he and the other kids in the neighbourhood were scared of her. Not because she was the neighbourhood's biggest gossip, which had most of the adults afraid of her, but because the kids were convinced she was some kind of genetically modified human experiment. Or a witch.

"Just keep her off of my lawn. I don't need her destroying my grass."

Justin and Ollie glanced at each other with wide eyes, not surprised by the cranky woman's demand. She put more effort into maintaining her grass than most people did keeping their jobs.

"Yes, Ma'am." Justin nodded, then ushered Ollie along with a gentle hand. Karma was already on the move to the next exciting thing to discover.

Brendon Garcia was just coming out his front door on his way to his job as a bus driver in the neighbouring city. "Hey, Ollie! Who's the good-looking girl with your dad?" The man slicked his medium-length black hair back, which, as far as Justin was concerned, was a textbook mobster hairstyle.

Oliver giggled, looking up at his dad. "Hi, Mr. Garcia. This is Karma. Are Tristan and Ed home?"

"Sure thing, kiddo. They're in the living room with Penny. Go on in and say hi." Brendon and his wife Anna had three children. Edward and Tristan were ten and nine, and their youngest, Penny, was just seven. The boys and Ollie were close friends.

Ollie glanced at his dad, asking permission with his eyes, so Justin nodded his approval before the boy darted off into the house.

Justin stepped toward Brendon. "She's a beauty, ain't she? Say hello to the newest member of the Suburban Watchdogs."

Brendon stared in Justin's direction for a moment, one eyebrow raised, creasing his forehead. "You got a dog to join our fake gang?"

"Fake? I'm as serious as a heart attack, Scar. Those fools struck again. We can't just sit around and do nothing." Justin was using every ounce of strength in his small frame to hold Karma back from jumping on Brendon. He would have failed had she not become distracted by a new arrival on the scene.

Morrie, AKA Whitey, pulled his rickety old work van into his driveway next door. His company logo for *Pest-o-cide*, the pest control business he worked for, was emblazoned across the sides. Karma was inexplicably drawn to him and started pulling Justin down the sidewalk.

"Wow, girl. Slow down!" Justin shouted as he sped down the sidewalk at a forty-five-degree angle. "Ollie? Karma and I are going next door. See ya 'round, Scar," he hollered behind him as Oliver darted out of the Garcia house to follow.

Karma jumped on Morrie and slobbered all over his work uniform. Morrie laughed and scratched her head as he encouraged her to get down. "Hello there. Who are you?" Despite not growing up with dogs, Morrie had always loved them. He'd have one of his own if it weren't for his wife's allergies. Morrie addressed Justin once the dog was settled beside him. "This is a beautiful Dogue de Bordeaux."

"Sorry, Whitey. Meet the newest member of the Suburban Watchdogs, Karma. She's not a wine dog though—whatever you said. She's a French mastiff."

Ignoring Justin's ignorance about dog breeds, knowing Scarlett had an affinity for Bordeaux wines, Morrie asked, "Are you serious? You got a dog for our fake gang?"

"It's not a fake gang! Why does everyone keep saying that? Those scumbags destroyed a local institution when they robbed *GoldenWood*. I'm not letting that slide."

"They struck again?"

"Heck yeah, and they did fifty Gs in damage. We have to do something."

"That's exactly why I pay my taxes, Fat Tony. We fund the police. They'll be much better suited to catching the bad guys than a bunch of exhausted dads."

A wide smile spread across Justin's face at hearing Whitey call him by his gangster name. His Fat Tony persona came into play, and he puffed out his chest to appear more intimidating. He could make a couple of opossums nervous. "Nah, man. They're stretched way too thin. We can't let our little town become a hub for criminal activity."

"You mean like a hot spot for gangs?" Morrie smirked, appreciating the irony in Justin's plan.

"Gangs are bad news. You don't want Jack or Alexis getting caught up in a gang."

"Jack is eight. I'm not worried about him being sucked into gang life." Morrie shook his head. "We've got to leave it to the professionals, man. We're not trained or equipped to take on criminals. Not to mention, none of us have the free time."

"You watched *Goodfellas*. You saw how easily a kid can get pulled into that life. Before you know it, Jack's in witness protection eating ketchup and egg noodles."

Morrie chuckled. "If I had a loonie for every time you said something smart, I wouldn't be able to buy a coffee."

"Tim Hortons or Starbucks?"

Morrie blinked his eyes at his small friend as he hesitated to answer. "Starbucks?"

"Aw, thanks, man." Justin blushed like he'd been paid a compliment but overlooked Morrie's jesting tone.

"Anyway," Morrie leaned down to scratch an eager Karma behind her ears. "You're a pretty girl. You don't look like you'll be much of a threat as a guard dog, though."

"That's where you're wrong. She's an excellent judge of character. I bet she'd tear a strip out of a bad guy if I gave her the word."

"And what word would that be?"

Justin leaned toward Morrie and whispered in his ear.

As Morrie attempted to repeat the word aloud, Justin placed a finger to his lips. "SHH. Don't say it. She'll go for your jugular."

"All right then. I'll take your word for it." Morrie was confident the dog wouldn't do any intentional harm. "I'll let you get on with your walk. Ollie looks like he's ready to go instead of listening to us old guys talk." He reached forward, rustling the toque on the young boy's head.

"It's fine, Mr. Morris."

Ollie was a good kid. He was polite and intelligent—one had to wonder if he was the mailman's son. If he didn't look like a miniature version of Justin, Ollie's paternity would have been up for debate amongst the neighbours. It was hard to believe he belonged to Scarlett, either. The woman came across as cold and stuck up—nothing like her son, or her husband, for that matter.

"Come on then Ollie, let's take Karma to the yard at the school and let her run around."

Morrie placed a hand on his friend's shoulder and gave him a tight smile. It was obvious Justin was trying to do all he could to keep his child happy despite the rocky relationship waiting at home. More than ever, Morrie was grateful for his wife, Nicole. "I'll see you later, Fat Tony."

Justin's eyes lit up again. Maybe his friends would come around to the idea after all. Somebody had to stop the criminals because when good people sat back and refused to take action, that's when the bad guys won.

No; no bad guys would be winning on Justin's watch. Especially not with Karma by his side.

Karma is coming.

DISTURBING THE PEACE

A t 6:30 on a Wednesday evening in late March, Justin was sitting on the living room floor of his home, tending to Karma, when his wife entered the room. She squirmed at the sight of the dog. It had been three weeks of dog ownership and Scarlett had yet to warm up to the idea.

"Do you really need to keep that *thing* in the living room? I don't want her hair and slobber all over the furniture."

Justin ignored his wife—something he'd become skilled at—but Scarlett continued her rant. "What are people going to think if they come over and leave covered in dog hair? Or what if the house starts smelling like a dog? That's a disgusting smell, Justin, and I won't tolerate it." Scarlett was pacing, flailing her arms about as she spoke. "Are you even paying attention to a word I say?"

"That's a weird way to start a conversation."

Scarlett was visibly angry, staring at Justin with narrowed eyes. Her dainty features had mastered the perturbed look several years ago. "There is something seriously wrong with you."

"That's a mean thing to say right before our dog's first yoga class!"

"Her what, now?" Scarlett's eyes widened as she jerked her head back. She stammered out her words but couldn't form a coherent sentence. "Her... her... yo... yoga?"

"Her yoga class. Your negativity is going to affect her vinyasa."

"You have *got* to be kidding me. How much is this costing us? You don't make enough money to be wasting it on stupid stuff."

"It was an online group discount coupon thing. Don't worry; I didn't spend your manicure money."

Karma wagged her tail as Scarlett stomped off toward the kitchen. She could be one of the few people who brought joy to a dog by leaving.

"Okay, my beautiful girl. Let's get you to your yoga class. I hope that tuna I fed you earlier doesn't make you gassy."

Justin and Karma arrived at *Clippendale's*, the local dog groomer with a yoga studio, twenty minutes early. The class was scheduled to begin at 7:30, so he had plenty of time to get Karma acclimated to the space.

Justin took a few moments to speak to the svelte, raven-haired instructor. "This is a nice place you have here, Donna."

"Oh, thank you, Mr. Peterson. I've tried to make it a comfortable space."

"Call me Justin. You're definitely older than me, anyway."

Donna's dark eyebrows pinched as she stared at the oblivious man. "Right. Thank you for pointing that out, Justin."

"My pleasure, Donna. Say, what are all these poles for in here?" Justin glanced around the room, taking in all the floor-to-ceiling chrome poles bolted in place. The rest of the decor appeared very zen, with stark white walls, birch wood floors, and potted plants throughout the room.

Donna looked at Justin again, head tilted, and brows pulled together. "Those are for... other classes we run."

Justin thought for a moment, looked down at Karma, then back up at Donna. "Ohh, I gotcha." He winked.

"Right, well, I better go get set up. I hope you enjoy the class, Mr. Peter... Justin."

"Thanks. I'm sure Karma is going to feel like a new dog after she's done here."

Without another word, Donna turned to walk away —at least not out loud. Her silent opinions on Justin were another matter.

Justin looked at Karma and whispered, "I wonder why they'd want to have a pole-dancing class for dogs. How would you hold on without thumbs?"

Even Karma tilted her head at her beloved owner.

"Well, let's find a place to roll out your yoga mat, Karm. We better get you ready." Justin looked around and realized he was the only man in a class full of women, and they were all in *Lululemon* or *Lolë* workout clothes. They were more Scarlett's crowd than Justin's, but he carried on getting set up. Karma was also the only dog that exceeded fifteen pounds; the rest of the dogs arrived inside purses. He shrugged his shoulders and spoke in a comforting tone to his dog, "Now, if you have to fart, don't be embarrassed. It's perfectly natural—especially in a yoga class. No one will think any less of you."

The women glanced over at him with serious expressions from their own yoga mats. Justin wondered to himself why all the other dogs were still in their purses. *They can't do yoga in a purse.*

Donna broke the chatter by getting the class's attention. "Good evening, everyone. Thanks again for joining us for *Dogs and Yoga*. If everyone can take their positions on their mats, we'll begin in a moment. Just take a few seconds to calm your breathing and really focus on what lies ahead for the next forty-five minutes."

"Did you hear that Karm? Calm your breathing. Stick your tongue back in your mouth and cool it on the drool. You're going to make your yoga mat slippery."

As she did best, Karma was seated beside Justin on the yoga mat, panting and drooling. She rested her massive head on his shoulder while he sat cross-legged, awaiting the start of the class. He didn't even flinch at the liquid soaking through his shirt because he was happy to have such a loyal girl. Karma had quickly become his favourite woman in the house, but he couldn't admit that to Scarlett. He reached his hand up to scratch under Karma's ear as she blew her hot breath in his at a steady pace. Though her fur was soft, her dog breath left a lot to be desired. Ignoring the fact that she smelled like a baby convention where they ran out of diapers, Justin leaned into her snuggles and tried to calm her for her yoga class.

"Okay, everyone," Donna interrupted the silence. "Let's get started. We're going to start in a standing position called mountain pose."

Justin looked at Donna as she stood with her feet together, palms together in front of her heart. He looked at Karma, then back at Donna. "Um, Donna? I don't know how to make Karma stand like that."

Donna already appeared exasperated. "Mr. Peterson; I'm sorry, Justin, *you* are supposed to stand. This is a dogs *and* yoga class, not a dog yoga class."

Oh. Well, that was an oversight. Justin tried to save himself some embarrassment by saying, "Of course, it's just... Karma wanted to join in, too."

"Sure. Well, maybe she can stand on four paws for mountain pose then, hmm? Can we get back to the class now?"

"Right. Sure thing. Of course. No problem," Justin stammered. *I guess I'm doing a yoga class. I wish I had brought Karma to the pole-dancing class instead.* He spent the next forty-five minutes struggling through various yoga poses while Karma made her way around the room, sniffing the purse-dog's butts. Considering Justin showed up in jeans and a long-sleeve flannel shirt, he managed pretty well, but it hadn't been nearly as much fun as the dog yoga he expected.

Once they completed the class and Karma fully embraced Shavasana with zero shame, Justin rubbed her belly and told her it was time to leave. She flopped over and got up onto all fours, then dropped her front half to the ground in a downward dog pose. "There you go, Karm! You're a natural! Do you see this Donna? She's a natural."

The other participants in the class looked over in Karma's direction, just in time for her to release a loud fart. The remaining women in the class looked at Justin, horrified, as if he were the offender. When Karma finished her stretch, Justin patted her on the head and urged her to leave. "Come on, girl. Let's get out of here before they realize that it wasn't just loud," he whispered.

41

Justin exited the front of *Clippendale's* with Karma walking closely beside him. Once the cool night air hit them both, Karma released a low growl with her hackles raised.

Nothing suspicious appeared in Justin's initial scan of the street. "What is it, girl?"

Karma's growling persisted as she watched the north side of the street where all the businesses appeared closed. There were no pedestrians on the sidewalk because it was still too cold for people to stroll along the streets with everything shut down for the night.

Justin called Karma toward his pickup truck and encouraged her to get in. She was hesitant to move from her guarded position, but her loyalty to her master won out. She hopped into the passenger seat and stuck her wrinkly face against the window, covering it with slobber art. Justin climbed into his seat and closed the door just as he heard a commotion on the street behind them.

A full-sized white work van skidded to a stop in front of the pharmacy, and two men came rushing out of the building. Before Justin could even comprehend what was happening, the van sped off in front of him. His instinct was to follow the van and call 911, but he knew making phone calls while driving was illegal—he couldn't report a crime while committing one. He opened the door, climbed out, and called for Karma to join him as he walked toward the pharmacy. He phoned the police on his way.

"911, what's your emergency?"

"I think there's been a robbery at the *LifeZest Pharmacy*. The suspects just took off toward the *Dairy Queen* in a big white van—two men plus a driver. I'm going inside to check if there are any victims."

"Sir, please don't enter the pharmacy. I am sending the police to your location immediately. Stay out of sight in case the perpetrators return."

"It's fine. I've got my dog with me, and she just did some yoga."

"Um, I'm not sure how that's relevant, but please, Sir, wait in a safe location. Is your vehicle nearby?"

"I was in my truck when I saw them take off. I'm going inside now."

"Sir—"

Justin ended the call.

ROBBERY

Justin walked up to the side of the pharmacy, which had an entire wall of windows at the front. He slowly leaned around the corner and placed his face up against the glass with his hands, shielding the reflection from the streetlights so he could see inside. There was no sign of anyone. He leaned his ear up to the glass to listen for any commotion. It would be a lot easier to hear without those sirens blaring in the background. Once he had determined there was no threat to his safety, Justin put on his Fat Tony courage and entered the building. The inconsiderate criminals hadn't locked the door upon leaving, so getting inside was easy.

The sirens were growing louder with each passing second, but Fat Tony carried on toward the back of the building. Behind the pharmacy counter was a middle-aged man with black hair, medium-brown skin, and terrified brown eyes—he'd been tied to a support beam at the edge of the shelving unit that housed the medications. The near-empty shelving indicated what the criminals were after. "Hey buddy, I'm here to help. Is there anyone else here?" The man shook his head. "Okay, the police are coming. I'm going to cut your hands loose."

The man nodded his approval.

"Police! Everybody put your hands up!"

Justin ignored the command because he was busy using his Swiss Army keychain knife to cut through the tape on the pharmacist's wrists. Karma was eagerly licking Justin's face as he bent over to help the man. Justin giggled at the tickly tongue assaulting his face. "Stop it, Karm. You're getting your goobers everywhere." Justin was struggling to cut the tape free from the employee, but Karma was relentless in showing her affection.

"I said put your hands up!" A voice boomed from in front of the counter.

"One second man, I almost have this tape free."

"You have two seconds to put your hands up."

Karma turned to face the constable with determination in her eyes. Before anyone could react, the hundred-pound dog lunged forward at the uniformed man, tackling him to the ground, and licked his face relentlessly.

"Karma, no. Karma, come."

Like a good dog, she returned to sit beside her master, but the constable was on his side spitting, trying to clean his face with his sleeve.

"Hey, I'm sorry about that, man. She just thinks everyone loves her. Are you all right?" Justin reached his hand out to help the man stand as other men and women in uniform rushed past to clear the scene.

The muscular blond man refused the helping hand and stood, giving Karma an intense glare. "That dog is a menace, and I told you to put your hands up! Don't make me tase you."

"Now there's no need for that. I'm just here to help." Justin looked at the cursive embroidered in the man's uniform to address him by name. "I was the one who called you guys, Constable Pee-cult."

The officer turned his narrowed grey eyes toward Justin. "It's Constable Picault, Pee-koe," he enunciated.

"Sorry about that. You should get someone to fix your nametag then. They spelled it wrong."

Picault released an exasperated sigh. "Just call me René then. What's your name?"

Justin stifled a laugh. "René? Isn't that a girl's name?"

"It's French. I assure you, it's a man's name." René stood taller to enhance his masculinity, which wasn't really necessary with his six-foot muscular frame.

"Oh, hey. My girl here is French too! That must be why she likes you so much." Justin looked down at his dog with a proud smile. She sat beside him, wagging her tail and producing a drool puddle on the floor.

It quickly became clear to René the level of intellect in the man before him. "Can you tell me your name, please?"

"It's Fat…" The small blond man shook his head. "Justin. Justin Peterson."

"What were you going to say?"

"Oh nothing. Fat… you have a fat head. Yeah, that's what I was going to say. You must be really smart. Maybe it's a French thing. Karma here has a fat head too, and she's the smartest girl I know."

Picault pinched the bridge of his nose, taking deep breaths to stop himself from being consumed by frustration. "Thanks for that."

"You know, they say dogs are as smart as a two-and-a-half-year-old kid, but not Karma. I think she's as smart as me."

"That seems about right. So, Mr. Peterson, what were you doing here?"

"I was at a dog yoga class at *Clippendale's*. Karma farted doing downward dog, so we high-tailed it out of there."

Somehow, that statement left Constable Picault with more questions than answers. "And, this dog yoga class, what time did you leave?"

"Right around 8:20. Karma and I walked outside, and she was staring at the pharmacy, growling. I told you she's smart. I thought it was just a raccoon or something, so I got her in the truck. A few seconds later a big white van skidded up and two guys jumped in."

"Did you catch the license plate number?"

"No, I didn't. Sorry, man."

"That's fine, Mr. Peterson. It's our job to catch these guys. Anything you can tell us would be helpful, though. Did the van have any business name or distinguishing marks?"

"Just a plain white van. No windows in the back. The one guy who ran outta here must have been near eight feet tall, though. He looked like Yao Ming's Irish body double."

"Who?"

"Yao Ming. Basketball player. Do they not have basketball in France?" Justin mimicked bouncing and throwing a basketball, as if clarification was needed. "Sorry, basket-boll."

"I'm from Montreal, not France. I'm just not familiar with Yao Ming."

"Ah, Montreal," Justin said with a terrible French accent. "Lovely place, Montreal. Home of the Wonderbra."

René released a frustrated sigh and held his hand to his temple with his eyes closed to keep himself calm. He took a few slow breaths.

Another officer from behind the counter, who was helping the employee, walked toward René. "You almost done here, Picault?"

"Almost. Give me a minute," René addressed his partner—a short, pale, stocky man with a receding hairline and no career ambitions. A stark contrast to

Picault, who wanted to uphold the promise he had made to keep the people of his new hometown safe, and took his physical health seriously. "Mr. Peterson— can you write your contact information here, please? Phone number, email, home address. We'll be in touch with any more questions."

"So, I'm not under arrest or anything?"

"Should you be?"

"Well, I didn't tackle you and kiss your face, so I guess not."

"Lucky for you, stupidity is not a crime. I see no valid reason to arrest you, but I'd suggest not entering a crime scene in the future."

"That's real nice of you, René. I don't think I'd survive long in prison."

René couldn't disagree with that statement, so he gave Justin a nod.

Justin then leaned in and whispered, "I have shy bowels, if you know what I mean."

Picault's nose scrunched as he wished he could rewind the last several minutes of his life and prevent the encounter from ever happening. "Unfortunately, I do. Thank you for your time, Mr. Peterson. We'll be in touch."

"Yep, no problemo, Constable René. You catch these guys."

"We'll do our best."

René breathed a sigh of relief as he watched the irritating short man vacate the building and head down the street.

49

Justin turned to leave the pharmacy with Karma at his side and got back in his truck. He couldn't wait to tell the other Suburban Watchdogs all about his experience at the next guys' night and put a plan in action.

CRIMINAL CONSPIRACY

Morrie was looking forward to another guys' night. After a long week of work, relaxing, watching the hockey game was exactly what he needed. He appreciated the Millers for opening their home each week so the exhausted dads could unwind.

Justin and Karma met up with Morrie on the sidewalk outside of their houses. Karma pounced on Morrie with a level of excitement she only seemed to exhibit around him.

"Hey there, girl." Morrie placed the dog's front paws back on the ground and scratched her head. "She's still jumping up on everyone?"

"Not everyone. Just most people," Justin replied with a shoulder shrug. "There's Scar. Let's go get our seats."

Morrie shook his head. There were six seats in Josh's basement, and four guys. There was hardly going to be a battle.

"Heya, Watchdogs, Karma," Brendon greeted with a nod of his head.

"Hey. She's not separate from the Watchdogs. She's just as much a part of this as we are." Justin kneeled down to Karma, rubbing her ears and allowing her to lick his face. "Don't let him make you think you're any less important, okay? You're my most special girl."

There's something to be said for the bond between a human and their dog, but Justin is dangerously skirting the line into weird.

"Let's go get our seats, then." Morrie walked to the Miller house, where he stepped onto the porch and rang the doorbell.

"I'm coming," Lily's voice called from inside. Ten seconds later, the door unlocked, and Lily swung it open, greeting the men with a smile. At least, until Karma pounced on her, knocking her to the floor and eliciting a shriek.

"Karma, no. Karma, come here," Justin shouted. "Gee, I'm sorry Lil. Are you all right?" He reached out to help her up.

Lily, a dainty blonde woman with blue eyes and fair skin, brushed off her clothing and used her sleeve to wipe the slobber off of her cheek. Karma had resumed her position sitting beside Justin, tongue lolled out of her mouth, wagging her tail like she was proud of herself for another successful tackle. She'd been practicing on Scarlett.

"What happened? Lily, are you okay?" Josh came huffing and puffing up the stairs.

"I'm fine. Karma just got over-excited. I'm pretty sure she nibbled my ear." Lily's nose scrunched up as she tilted her head and shrugged a shoulder to clean off her ear.

"Oh yeah, she loves doing that. You gotta love her. Everyone needs a little romance sometimes." The laughter that bubbled out of Justin after that statement had Morrie concerned that Justin had well passed that line into weird.

Everyone else in the room was left staring at Justin, questioning his standard for romance. Even Brendon, who wanted to buy his wife an oil change for their anniversary.

"Justin, you've got to keep your dog in line. She's really going to hurt someone," Morrie, ever practical, advised.

"She's just trying to love everyone. If she wants to hurt you, you'll know."

"Unless you want a lawsuit on your hands, you need to keep her under control. It's not good for her to be jumping on everyone."

"Her last owner said she was a jumper. I read that jumping is a normal part of a dog's greeting routine."

The other three men and Lily looked stunned for a moment. Brendon broke the silence and said what everyone was thinking. "You read?"

"Yeah, I read! What do you all think I'm stupid or something?"

"I don't think you're stupid," Brendon replied. "You just have bad luck... with thinking... and speaking."

"If it weren't for bad luck, I'd have no luck at all." Justin toed off his shoes, setting them to the side of the entryway mat. "Anyway, we're going to miss the game if we stand here lollygagging. I'm sorry about Karma's excitement, Lily, but you should feel good because she's an excellent judge of character... Well, except she's always doing the same thing to Scarlett."

"I'm flattered," Lily deadpanned.

Before the game started, Morrie went to use the restroom as the other men got settled in for the game. When he entered the man cave, he walked in on a conversation in progress and wasn't sure what he'd missed that would help the story make sense.

"No joke. If she hadn't farted right at that moment, we would have missed the whole thing."

"Or if she farted sooner, you could have stopped the robbery in progress," Brendon replied.

"Every time I think our conversations couldn't possibly get weirder, you guys kick it up a notch," Morrie chimed in. He walked over to the basement bar's mini fridge to grab a beer. As he set four beer cans on the counter and continued, "Please explain to me whose fart could have stopped a robbery in progress and remind me to never stand behind her."

"No, man. Her fart couldn't stop a robbery." Justin rolled his eyes. "I took Karma to a dog yoga class. She farted doing downward dog, so we ran out of there before the stink hit us. She had tuna for dinner, so I knew it was gonna be a bad one. When I got outside of *Clippendale's*, those same guys were robbing the pharmacy. They took off in a van, then I called 911 and ran into the store to check for victims. I'm telling you, these guys are ruthless, and the cops didn't seem too concerned about it. Heck, the cop I talked to doesn't even know who Yao Ming is!"

The men were all in shock. Josh spoke for the others, "How could anyone not know who the seven-foot-six basketball player is? He is basically a walking tree who was featured on any sports news channel for over a decade. Is this cop a joke?"

"I know. He was totally clueless. He even threatened to tase me while I was getting the tape off of the pharmacy guy. The nerve."

"So, what did they say?" Josh prompted Justin for more details.

"Just that they'd try to catch the guys. I'm not too confident, though. He's probably a *Canadiens'* fan. They have bad judgement."

The guys sat in relative silence for the next forty minutes, watching the first period of the hockey game. The *Maple Leafs* were playing the *Senators*, so it was always a high stakes game—Ontario hockey pride was on the line. The odd cheer or grumble was expressed, but their earlier conversation had been put to rest while the game was on.

At the start of the first intermission with the game tied one-one, Justin looked at his friends and felt confidence bloom in his chest. "We have to stop these guys. They're going to terrorize the whole town. We can't just sit back."

"Justin, we don't have the skill set or the resources to track down criminals. What would we even do if we caught them?" Morrie asked.

"Citizen's arrest."

"Justin is right, Morrie. They're going to ruin our town. Everyone will be living in fear, and more criminals will move their way in. It's a slippery slope." Josh walked toward the bar to fill up a bowl of chips. Lily insisted eating out of the bag was for Neanderthals when you have company, so a proper bowl is a must. Happy wife, happy life.

"Guys, we have to trust the police to handle the situation. We can't be rolling out like the Avengers. If I had an Ironman suit, I'd be game, but my exterminator gear isn't going to cut it."

"We don't need Ironman suits. We'll make our own uniforms. We aren't taking on Thanos—just a tall dude and his little friends. We won't be in any danger."

"You're really calling them little friends when you barely hit five-five with shoes on?" Morrie thought to himself if he did push ups instead of eye rolls every time Justin surprised him, he'd be in excellent shape.

"Well, they're little compared to the tall guy—and Thanos."

"It doesn't matter how big they are if they have guns. They're robbing stores. I doubt they show up with a whistle and a Yo-Yo. We should leave it to the police. Now they know something about what the guys look like and what they're driving." Morrie scanned the room and looked at each of his friends, but they all looked disappointed. So be it. He wasn't about to risk his life to stop criminals he knew nothing about. There was a snowman's chance in hell he'd get involved in this stupidity.

"So do we! I saw the van and the guys. Maybe I have that...what do you call it... picture memory?"

"Photographic memory," Morrie corrected as he made a mental note to do a pushup later.

"Right, photographic memory. Maybe as soon as I see them, I'll recognize them, and we can get these criminals out of our town. We'd be heroes. We'd probably have our picture in the paper and get a key to the city."

Push up. "They don't give out keys to the city— especially not to people interfering in ongoing criminal investigations. If anything, we'd probably be charged with obstruction of justice, and I don't make enough money to hire a lawyer. I'm out."

"Don't be a pansy, Whitey! The least we can do is just keep an eye out and if we see anything suspicious, we'll go from there. As long as we have each other's backs, we'll be fine." Josh was trying to be the voice of reason amongst the group. His motivation to keep the town his wife and kids live in safe was all he needed to be convinced. "I don't want Lily or my girls to be afraid to go to the grocery store or the pharmacy. If I can keep that from happening, you're darn right I will."

Morrie gave it some thought and considered the perspectives of his friends. With or without him, it seemed that they were poised to take on the bandits, so the least he could do was have their backs. Against his better judgement, he uttered three words that had Justin ready to kiss him: "Suburban Watchdogs: Assemble."

SECRET COMMISSIONS

Morrie was busy getting his kids ready for school on a Monday morning. Alexis was seven, and in the same grade as Josh's daughter Dahlia and Brendon's daughter Penny. It was a mystery when sending your kids to school became more work for parents than for kids. Between getting them dressed, packing lunches, dropping them off, the endless fundraisers, class trips, and homework, it was like a part-time job. Morrie was happy to do whatever it took to help his kids get an education, though, so he made an effort to split the school duties with his wife, Nicole.

Nicole walked downstairs as Morrie was struggling to style Alexis' hair. The sight made Nicole erupt in laughter.

"Daddy, it's too tight! I can't blink my eyes."

"Let me help you, Wesley. You finish getting Jack ready." Nicole's chuckles subsided as she walked over to fix her daughter's hair.

"You are my queen." He leaned in to kiss his wife's cheek. When they were married, beyond the typical vows, he made a promise to always make her feel valued and appreciated. He remained a man of his word.

Nicole chuckled as she took the hairbrush from Morrie's hand and gave him a peck on the cheek in return. He grunted in approval because, even after twelve years of marriage, they were still very much in love. Nicole was a pretty, curvy woman with bronze skin and hazel eyes, which gave her a unique appearance that captivated anyone who looked in her direction. Her curly hair was soft and luscious, which she'd always kept natural. Her skin was flawless, so she was confident without makeup, and that gave her an effortless beauty. Beyond her physical appearance, she had always been a wonderful wife and mother, and helped anyone in need. She worked as a medical office assistant, and her co-workers and patients had nothing but kind things to say about her. Morrie looked at his wife brushing his daughter's hair and decided at that moment he had made the right decision to help his friends keep their town safe. He couldn't stomach his family being in danger, knowing he could have tried to stop it.

Once Jack was dressed in his spring gear and ready to head off to school, Nicole slid on her coat and shoes to walk them down the road. The school was only a kilometre away, so often the children of the neighbourhood walked to and from as a group. As long as the Suburban Watchdogs could keep Alliston safe from any further dangers, the young friends could keep doing so, but for the time being, at least one parent escorted them.

Morrie kissed everyone goodbye and wished them all a great day, then he rushed upstairs to get on his uniform and gather what he needed for another eight to ten hours of facing off against renegade raccoons and mice. He didn't mind the four-legged creatures, but when it came to bats or cockroaches, that was another story. Being an exterminator—or as the company website put it, a "wildlife relocation specialist", even though sometimes they were relocated to the afterlife—was never supposed to be a long-term gig, but the pay was decent, and the work was steady, so as a man with a young family, it had provided what they needed.

Rushing out the door, Morrie spotted Justin walking Karma up the street. The snow had mostly melted, which should bring excitement for warmer weather, but the streets looked dirty as the melted snow exposed the trash and dog poop deposited over the winter. Morrie waved toward Justin, happy to see the dog on a leash, but she was pulling Justin so hard down the street, she practically flew him like a kite. Before Morrie could slide into his work van and leave, Justin ran across the street into the driveway. Whether he wanted to was a different issue, because Karma hadn't given him a choice.

"Whitey? Hey, Whitey! I'm glad I caught you. I just wanted to let you know I'm going to go over to *Canadian Tire* today and get us some supplies for our mission."

"Justin, I swear if you come back with a crossbow, I'm going to shoot you with it."

"Woah, man. No need to get violent. I'm not getting murder weapons—I've already got Karma."

Morrie stifled a laugh. He watched Karma coddle a docile bumblebee two days earlier. The dog didn't have an ounce of violence in her hundred-pound frame. "All right then. I'll leave you to pick up whatever you think we'll need, but nothing too expensive. We're all scraping by as it is, and you know Brendon will have a fit over spending anything."

"The ol' cheapskate. There's no price too steep for keeping our town safe. Before I forget, do you have a black polo shirt and khaki pants?"

"I'm pretty sure I do, but they won't fit you." Morrie scanned Justin's petite frame and tried to picture him wearing clothes made for his own six-foot, 200-pound body.

"Not for me, Whitey. For you. That's what we're going to wear as our uniforms because Brendon wouldn't agree to me choosing something else."

Curiosity took over, and Morrie couldn't help but ask, "What was your other suggestion?"

"Here, I'll show you." Justin pulled up the Suburban Watchdogs' Amazon wish list on his phone, which had flashlights, protein bars, binoculars, and memory foam slippers. He stopped scrolling as he reached his selection. The sheer excitement in his eyes was almost endearing if it were anything else he was excited about.

"*Ninja Turtles*?"

"Well, can you think of a better group of four guys who stop crime?" Justin raised his eyebrows and held one hand on his hip with Karma's leash looped on his wrist. "I tried to get *Power Rangers* so Karma could be the pink one, but I couldn't find one to fit her."

Morrie imagined four grown men wandering the town in *Ninja Turtle* or *Power Ranger* suits and couldn't suppress a laugh. Throw in Karma in her Kimberly Hart outfit, and they'd have been quite a sight. Especially since the costumes were made in China and deemed "one size fits all." It was a virtual guarantee Justin would walk around looking like he was wearing pyjamas, while Morrie would look like he squeezed into a scuba suit. "That's too bad Brendon wouldn't go for it, man. It was a good idea." Morrie tried to play it off, so he didn't have to be the realistic one to crush Justin's dream for once. If there was one thing he was confident about, it was Brendon's unrelenting cheapness.

"I'll see if I can talk him into it. He might come around. In the meantime, dig out your pants and shirt. We'll make that work for now."

"Will do. I better get going. I'll see you at guys' night."

"I'll have all our gear by then and we can get a plan into action. Let's just hope these guys don't strike again before then."

Friday arrived, and Morrie walked toward Josh's house and was welcomed inside by Lily. He had always appreciated the woman's support of their weekly guys' night and made it a point to thank her for all she did to accommodate them. As much as he and his neighbours were opposites in a lot of ways, he had grown to enjoy their friendship. It helped that their kids and wives got along so well—minus Scarlett. Their friendships gave the neighbourhood a real sense of community—one that deserved protecting.

Morrie ambled downstairs, meeting the remaining three-quarters of his street crew, and entered a heated conversation happening over a game of chess.

"I'm not wearing a *Ninja Turtle* costume, Justin," Josh stated. "You think anyone named Fat Tony would be caught dead in that?"

"Why not? People take them seriously. As soon as the Ninja Turtles show up, you know something is about to go down," Justin replied.

"Not happening. This isn't a comic book. I'll do my part trying to stop these guys, but I'm not dressing like no mutant amphibian."

"Is that a person who can write with both hands?"

Morrie stifled a groan. Add another push up to the tally. "That's ambidextrous."

"Oh, right." Justin nodded. "Don't you think it's weird we have one hand that does everything and the other one's just there… can't even sign your name?"

Josh closed his eyes and scratched his right eyebrow. "No, I never thought about it before."

From the sofa, Brendon chimed in, "Morrie's here. Can we have beer now?"

"Yeah, help yourself." Josh looked across the chess board at Justin. "What do you say we make this game interesting?"

"Good idea." He slid his chair back, stood, and walked away from the table.

"Where are you going?"

"I thought you wanted to make it interesting. Leaving is the only way to do that."

Josh grumbled something unintelligible. He caught Morrie's shoulders shaking in silent laughter. "I was going to make a wager. If I won, he'd scrap the *Ninja Turtles* costume idea. He's a dog with a bone."

Morrie's laughter was silent no longer. His booming laugh drew the attention of the other two men across the room.

Brendon shouted, "What's so funny over there?"

"Josh wants to get Karma a bone." Morrie schooled his expression, regaining composure. He'd been a victim of Justin's idiocy on more occasions than he could count, but it never got old seeing other people have to deal with it.

Karma's head lifted and her ears quirked from her perch on the sofa. She'd already claimed her seat.

"That's nice of you. She loves them things. Scarlett is losing her mind over all the holes in the backyard, but I don't have the heart to tell Karma no."

Josh sent Morrie a glare, reigniting his silent laughter.

The men sat down for an evening watching The Godfather II, having no sporting events of interest on. Fat Tony came out in full force after a couple of drinks and started quoting Don Vito Corleone word for word. It made for an interesting, albeit irritating, movie-watching experience. He was unbothered by Karma's head on his shoulder, soaking his shirt with her drool. Personal space was not a concept the dog understood, but Justin didn't seem to mind.

"So, how are we going to set out our stakeout schedule?" Justin asked during a break from parroting the movie.

"My brother is coming on Sunday, but other than that, I'm free on the weekend." Josh was the first to reply, excitement gleaming in his eyes.

"My weekend is clear, but I work evenings all next week." Brendon grabbed some of the residual popcorn kernels and shoved them in his mouth—aside from the ones he dropped on the front of his argyle sweater.

Morrie was hesitant to make any effort to encourage their vigilante mission, but he felt obligated to follow through. "My weekend is clear too, but I doubt they're going to strike in the middle of a Saturday."

"All we know so far is that they drive a big white van, and one guy is a hundred feet tall. How are we supposed to watch for them?" Josh asked.

Justin's eyes lit up in the way they do when he thought he had a great idea. "I'll draw a sketch." He got up from his spot, walked over to the Miller girls' arts and crafts station in the opposite corner of the basement, and took out some pencil crayons.

Morrie glanced at the other two men watching Justin sit in a tiny child's chair and not look out of place. "This oughtta be good."

Ten minutes later, Justin returned with a sketch of two men and a deformed van.

"That looks like something you drew with your left hand," Josh stated.

"I did. I was practicing to be amphibi-dextrous."

"Ambidextrous," Morrie clarified, trying but failing to keep his laughter at bay.

The three other men gathered around Justin's drawing and took in the details of the two men. One was the full length of the page, had a receding hairline of short 'Mango Tango' hair with touches of 'Timberwolf', a scowling face, and bulging blue eyes. He also had unruly eyebrows, but it was hard to tell if that was an intentional choice, or from drawing with the wrong hand. The second man only reached to the tall man's armpit and had a similar expression, wild, medium brown hair—perhaps the colour 'Beaver'—angry brown eyes, and facial hair.

"Aside from the one guy being tall, these look like any average guy in town," Brendon remarked.

"Nah. Trust me. You'll know when you see them. No doubt about it." Justin handed the drawing to Morrie, who inspected it more closely.

His artistic abilities were not going to win any awards, but Morrie was able to get the gist of what the men looked like. It might not work on a nightly news report to cast a wider net to recognize the criminals, but it would help the Watchdogs narrow their search.

Starting the next day, the hunt was on.

FORCIBLE ENTRY

All systems were a go. The heist crew's next target was chosen, and all that was left was last-minute recon. Their last job had a bit of a hiccup and the cops showed up a few minutes after they escaped, but luckily, they were too far behind to cause any issues. When the men arrived back at their temporary accommodations, they agreed it was time to ditch the van already. Someone had to have seen them, and that just wouldn't do. Thankfully, they had already replaced the one with the stupid beaver on the side before that last job.

Unfortunately, Rodney had nothing else big enough to transport Gord around, so they had to take their chances by keeping the van a while longer. It would have been more of a risk trying to squeeze Gord into a Prius than using a compromised van. The good news was, the Ram van was generic, and they covered the license plates, so it should be hard to identify.

On the agenda was to do some surveillance of their next target, which they'd hit in a few weeks. Downtown Alliston was not busy in the evenings, so the best opportunity to blend in was the middle of the day, while everything was open. People were always so caught up in getting through their daily tasks, they never paid attention to others around them. Ignorance allowed people like Gord, Nelson, and Earle to go unnoticed.

Gord and Earle got in the van and drove into town. Scouting a location didn't require three guys, and two guys in a van looked like co-workers—which, of course, they were; they just weren't your average blue-collar workers. Nah, those guys were suckers. Slaves. Spending their days busting their butts to earn a paycheck barely big enough to pay for a roof over their heads. That was a life Gord would never settle for, criminal record or not.

"What do you reckon we'll make from this score? I hope we can hit 50Gs." Earle rubbed his hands together, bobbing his head from side to side. "That would set us up good to make this stop our last before we retire."

Although Gord was sure retirement was the best course of action—quit while you're ahead—he also found himself worried that he'd be bored, unstimulated. They had worked hard to build up their nest egg and set themselves up for an easy life during their golden years, with no concerns over money, as long as they lived modestly. The biggest concern was having enough money for the endless supply of sunscreen Gord was sure to need. But was that what he wanted to do with himself? Only time would tell.

He put those concerns on the back burner and focused on the task at hand. "We should make 75Gs easy on this one. We just have to be smart about it. The pharmacy job was too close for comfort."

"That was weird. I checked all businesses on the street's hours beforehand and the only ones that were open were the pharmacy and the dog groomer. They were running some weird uppity mom class, but it said online it finished at 8:30. Do ya think maybe one of the people in the apartments saw us and called it in?"

"Who knows? Whoever it was, we need to watch each other's backs and be careful. Especially since we're still driving this God-forsaken van. Rodney better find us something else fast."

"In this town, these white vans are sitting in every third driveway. No one's going to bat an eye at us. Don't get yourself worked up."

"Yeah, let's hope so. We're just scoping the place out today, anyway. We shouldn't give anyone reason to suspect us. Double check the alarm system, test our signal jammer on their security cameras, and study entry and exit points."

"Sure thing, boss man." Earle bent forward to slide on a special pair of prosthetic gloves that looked like normal hands—without Earle's trademark knuckle fur. They were a luxury purchase to prevent them from leaving fingerprints, but also avoid looking suspicious. "Remember how nervous we were on the first job we pulled together?"

Gord recalled the heist that landed his old friend in a world of trouble. The result wasn't ideal, but they learned more from the failings of that job than they ever had from successful ones. Earle's time in jail allowed him plenty of opportunity to connect with other career criminals and learn what got them caught. He emerged from his incarceration with a wealth of knowledge, familiar with what to do and not to do. One fellow prisoner taught him all about alarm systems and how to deactivate them efficiently—a skill he had not only become proficient at but put to good use.

Another man explained how he was busted because a little girl thought he was Santa Claus and a mob of kids surrounded him. He was left standing just outside of a big box store with a bag of stolen goods right as the police arrived. From that, Earle learned to never overlook potential threats.

Every prisoner had something to teach, and Earle had the right kind of personality to endear himself to even the most hardened criminal. He was a stereotypical con man, skilled at playing people against themselves. He had never cut hair in his life—and his hair often looked as if there were a family of birds living in it—but he convinced the other inmates he was a barber so they'd come to him and spill their guts with barbershop talk. It worked like a charm. He even became pretty decent at cutting hair with the dull tools he had available.

Earle's proficiency at blending in any situation, manipulating people to do his bidding, and his ability to deactivate alarm systems, made him a valuable member of the team.

Since his release six years earlier, they'd taken on that knowledge and created a virtually flawless criminal enterprise, amassing a small fortune, leaving chaos in their wake, and didn't have the slightest concern for the people they hurt.

They were about to.

Justin and Brendon, AKA Fat Tony and Scar, were walking down the south side of the main street while Whitey and Corky drove around town looking for anything suspicious. Since Fat Tony knew what the criminals looked like, and considering the ringleader looked like an aged leprechaun on growth hormones, spotting them wouldn't take a genius. Good thing.

"Who'd have thought a few months ago that we'd be spending our days off patrolling town looking for a bunch of wise guys." Scar adjusted his jacket, unzipping it to expose his rounded midsection.

"Just imagine what would have happened if we watched *Mrs. Doubtfire* instead of *Goodfellas* that night."

Both men stopped walking for a moment. Fat Tony imagined what inspiration would have struck if they had watched Robin Williams sporting fake knockers and a prosthetic nose instead of the gangster movie they had settled on. He considered for a moment that *Mrs. Doubtfire* could be a Suburban Watchdog uniform idea to make them inconspicuous. No one would suspect an old lady of anything. He could have been Mildred instead of Fat Tony. Anyone named Mildred would be viewed as harmless.

"Don't even think about it, man."

"What?" Fat Tony rattled his head and focused his eyes on his partner in anti-crime.

"I saw your wheels turning. None of us are dressing up like *Mrs. Doubtfire*."

With a hand held to his chest, Fat Tony replied, "I'm hurt you wouldn't even consider the idea. Is this because you're too cheap to pay for a wig?"

Scar stared at Fat Tony a moment, not giving away anything with his expression. "No. I'm not buying a wig, but it has nothing to do with being sensible with my money. You say cheap; I say smart."

"Fine. I just want people to take us seriously."

Scar snickered. "I don't think cross-dressing as an old lady is the way to make that happen. Normal clothes are a better option."

The Watchdogs continued walking and talking about life—a little of this, a little of that—when they observed a large white van driving slowly down the main street. Fat Tony shouted with excitement, slapping Scar's shoulder as he watched the van fifty yards ahead. Scar, being the more sensible of the two, grabbed his friend's arm to drag him inside the nearest open business. They stepped into a bookstore, appropriately named *Run for Cover*.

They stood directly inside the door so they could watch out the window, as Scar took out his phone to text their friends.

Scar: *Spotted. Perps parked on the main street by the bookstore.*

The van pulled over to park next to the curb in front of two banks.

Justin was standing on the window ledge, face pressed to the glass. "What do you think they're doing? They're not going to rob a bank, are they?"

A throat cleared behind the men, and they turned to see a not-so-friendly face belonging to a bookstore employee. "Can I help you with something?" Her voice didn't mask her irritation the slightest bit.

Gee. Whatever happened to customer service? With his best effort to think quickly, Justin replied, "I'm looking for a book by Shakespeare."

The lady, clearly not convinced, opted to play along. "Okay. Which one?"

Justin, who had turned back to watch out the window, stated with confidence he had no business expressing, "William."

The portly woman grumbled something indiscernible. "No, which book by *William* Shakespeare?"

"Oh, uh… How 'bout you pick your favourite and I'll buy it?"

The men returned to watching through the window, studying the white van. There were no signs of movement, and neither of the passengers exited the vehicle. It appeared they were doing their own recon.

Moments later, the sound of a throat clearing again interrupted the Watchdogs' efforts. The woman passed Justin a worn paperback copy of *King Lear* with a pleased smirk.

"Ah, *King Lear*. A tale of how both figurative and literal blindness can lead to one's destruction."

Brendon's and the bookstore employee's jaws dropped.

"You know, this is probably my favourite of Shakespeare's tragedies," Justin confirmed, slapping the paperback in his palm and fanning the pages with a satisfied smile.

Brendon stumbled over his words. His attention had moved from the white van to his friend's face.

Justin, sensing the question in his friend's glare, answered the unspoken words. "My grade eleven English teacher was this good-lookin' broad, so I tried real hard to impress her. Ended up impressing Scarlett instead. Look where that landed me."

"Scarlett's not all bad."

"The other night she got mad because I fell asleep on the couch with Karma. When I went up to bed, she woke from a dead sleep to go on about how I like the dog more than her. The woman whipped a pillow at me when I agreed." Justin shook his head. "Talk about mixed signals. Does she want me to be honest or not?"

"You told your wife… the woman you've been married to for fifteen years… that you like the dog more than you like her, and you don't understand why she was upset?" Brendon scrubbed his hands over his face. "Some things are better left unsaid, man. You should have read Miranda Rights instead of your wedding vows."

"I was just telling the truth. If she wasn't as vicious as a rabid dog, maybe I'd like her more."

Silence passed for a moment before Brendon spoke again. "This is a chicken and the egg situation."

Justin tilted his head, awaiting clarification.

"Did your wife turn into a raging monster first? Or did you turn into an oblivious airhead first?" Brendon's lips curved into a smirk. "Never mind. The egg came first."

The pair continued to watch out the window after pleading with the crotchety bookstore employee to allow them to stay, and they waited for their friends to arrive before deciding what to do. The crooks hadn't exited their van and appeared to be chatting amongst themselves. Fat Tony was itching for some action and anxiously awaited the men slipping up so they could swoop in and get them off of their streets.

Alas, it was not the day for such an accomplishment. With no apparent rhyme or reason, the white van pulled onto the road and drove away.

Whitey and Corky pulled up to the curb a few buildings west of the bookstore, but by that time, the white van was gone. They exited Corky's work van just as Scar and Fat Tony were walking out of the bookstore—Fat Tony with a *Run For Cover* bag in hand. *Guarantee, that's an Avengers comic in that bag*, Whitey thought.

"You just missed them. They never got out of the van, and we only saw two of them. I wrote a partial plate number, but I bet it's stolen." Justin was flailing his empty hand around, talking in an Italian accent. Fat Tony had come to play.

Morrie bit his bottom lip to stop himself from chuckling because his small friend looked more intense than ever. "We should report what you guys saw to the police."

"Why?" Justin looked confused—so, Justin looked like everyday Justin. "They can't do anything. The guys didn't do nothin' wrong, so tellin' 'em we saw a suspicious van parked by the bank with no idea if or when they'll strike isn't going to do any good."

The other two men nodded in agreement.

"Fat Tony's right. That's why we started this— because the cops are spread too thin and can't waste time on stakeouts with no information. We've got to keep an eye out for these guys ourselves." Corky won himself the admiring stare of Fat Tony who appeared enamoured by his friend's support.

"Corky knows where it's at, Whitey. We'll stake the place out ourselves and call for backup when the time comes."

Morrie glanced across the street at the banks, noticing all the people coming in and out, some shoving wads of cash into their wallets as they walked out the door. People of this town felt safe despite the recent spike in crime, but if he could help put a stop to fear from overtaking his townspeople, then he'd be a coward not to. "Fine. We'll watch the place for a few nights, but never alone. If we can't work out a schedule to come together, we'll just have to take our chances and have no one on watch. We need to live our lives too, so we can do our part, but I'm not taking on another full-time job."

"Badda-bing, badda-boom." Fat Tony fired his finger guns around, sporting a face-splitting smile. "That's what I wanna hear, Whitey. Good on ya."

"Badda-bing, badda-boom?"

Fat Tony pinched his fingers together, kissing them in an obnoxious, stereotypical Italian gesture. "That's the only Italian I know. Let's get back to headquarters and sort out a schedule for this week." With that, he turned around and walked back toward the other end of the street, where his pickup truck was parked.

"Headquarters?" Whitey mouthed to his friends standing in front of him.

They all chuckled, and Scar jogged away to catch up with Fat Tony, who appeared to have a renewed passion for stopping the town's swindlers.

BURGLARY

Once the Watchdogs had a guess as to the criminal's next target, they committed to staking the place out. In teams of two, they arranged their schedules so that most evenings, they could monitor the banks, and were poised to call 911 as soon as they saw something suspicious. At least, that was Whitey's plan, but he wasn't there; Fat Tony had other ideas.

Seventeen days after spotting the bandits on the main street, Fat Tony, Corky, and Karma were parked down the road from the banks, on the same side of the street so they could keep the minivan pointed in the right direction. They opted to bring Scarlett's blue minivan so they could keep a low profile. Fat Tony's truck and Corky's construction van were too suspicious and identifiable considering it was after 1am and the streets were otherwise deserted. The fact Karma was slobbering and shedding all over the immaculate minivan interior didn't bother Justin in the least. One couldn't say the same for Scarlett's reaction when she discovered it.

The guys were talking about random things—sports, work, kid's upcoming school events—when suddenly, an alarm started blaring down the street. With nothing more than streetlights lit up, they couldn't pinpoint which bank had been targeted, and no other vehicles were on the road. Fat Tony worried they'd miss their chance, and the criminals would escape from the back of the building. Rather than drive around to the rear entrance, Fat Tony hopped out of the van, pressing the button to open the rear door, and released Karma.

"Go get 'em, girl." He issued the command to the world's friendliest guard dog, and jogged along behind her, grateful he did that yoga class last month to get in better shape. Who knew chasing criminals would be so physically demanding?

Instead of running behind the bank, Karma darted across the street, down an alleyway between the bookstore and a politician's office.

Fat Tony whisper-shouted at the dog, "Karma. Karma! Where are you going?" To his surprise, she didn't reply, so he shrugged his shoulders and set off in the direction she went. Before he ventured off into the darkness after his favourite girl, he turned to his friend. "Corky, you stay here in case they come out of the bank. The cops are probably on their way because of the alarm, but we can't let them get away."

With a sheen of sweat accumulating over Corky's straight ash brown eyebrows, he nodded in agreement with Fat Tony. He had his cellphone in hand and waved to show that he was ready to do his part. "Sure thing. I'll stay here in the shadows and call 911 if I see anything happening over here."

"Watchdogs: Assemble," Fat Tony declared as he ran off into the dark

Karma was no longer in Fat Tony's sights, so he worried his loyal companion was off facing the bad guys alone. He grabbed the bear mace from his belt holster, ready to pull the trigger should the need arise. He tiptoed along the back of the Member of Parliament's headquarters, inching his way around dumpsters, fire escape ladders, and neglected shrubbery before he found himself standing behind a jewellery store with Karma sitting patiently, wagging her tail.

"What have ya got there, girl?"

Gord, Nelson, and Earle planned this heist to a tee. They knew exactly what to grab for the best score. They disarmed the alarm system, knew their escape routes, ETA for police to show up, everything. They

staked the place out twenty-four hours a day in shifts over the previous week to determine the best time to hit it, and they'd never been so confident.

Confidence could be costly.

Something went wrong. Whether Earle failed to disarm the alarm system properly, or one piece they picked up had its own individual alarm, none of them knew, but what they did know was that the alarm was loud and bound to attract attention.

"Grab your loot and haul ass. We gotta get out of here," Gord shouted to his counterparts through his black ski mask. He was sweating like a long-tailed cat in a room full of rocking chairs. He thought they had done enough jobs that they had learned the ins and outs. They're skilled enough, their risks should have been minimal. They planned well enough, their contingency plans had contingency plans. But none of those plans involved the alarm going off. That was a given. A foregone conclusion that Earle would eliminate the alarm without issue.

Nelson and Earle didn't need Gord to tell them what to do the second the ear-searing alarm sounded. They did one final arm sweep, scooping as much as they could into their bags, and turned for the back exit.

The three of them ran through the small space, shouting over each other about who failed to do their job right, but struggling to hear each other over the sound blaring in their ears. They stopped at the door to listen for commotion on the other side, not wanting to walk into an ambush, and once they were satisfied the coast was clear, they opened the door to rush into the darkness.

Gord took the lead, heading back to their cargo van with Earle and Nelson trailing behind. The man might be approaching fifty, but his long limbs provided an advantage neither of the other guys had. The van was parked seventy feet away, and Gord ate up that distance in just a few strides. The alleyway was dimly lit by a few neighbouring security lights and the full moon overhead, so they had to be cautious without losing time. In moments like those, every second counted.

As Gord opened the driver's door, tossing his bag of loot inside, he heard Nelson shout, followed by a thud.

"Woah, doggy. Hey, there. Where did you come from?" Nelson's voice was shaking as he addressed the massive dog that tackled him to the ground. He quickly understood the dog was only trying to lick his face. Nelson didn't mind dogs, but he didn't like them enough that he wanted a strange one licking his face; especially not when he was fleeing the scene of a crime.

Gord and Earle came running around the van and found Nelson on the ground, arms over his face, trying to fend off an eager dog's tongue. They were equal parts irritated and relieved.

"Shoo. Get out of here, you mangy mutt! Scram!" the big man yelled. The dog didn't rush off, but she unpinned Nelson and allowed him to get up. The bandits scrambled into the van while eyeing the dog, not willing to turn their backs on her. Once they were safely inside, they burned rubber, flinging up loose gravel in the alleyway as they made their escape.

"Where the hell did that dog come from? I didn't even hear her coming, and next thing I knew, I was on the ground. For a second, I thought I was a goner."

"She must be a missing dog. She had a collar, but no one else was around. You're just lucky she was friendly," Earle replied.

"I don't know if I'd call being tackled and slobbered on lucky, but better than having my throat ripped out." Nelson rubbed the sleeve of his black hoodie over his face, making noises of disgust. "That stupid dog licked my tonsils." He tried to compose himself, and in the process, made a discovery. "Dammit. I dropped my bag."

Gord nearly slammed the brakes at Nelson's realization but thought better of it when he remembered why he was driving like a felon on the run. "What do you mean you dropped your bag?" Gord seethed through gritted teeth.

"Gee, Gord. What do you think I mean? I *mean* my ears were ringing from the damn alarm EARLE here didn't disarm, so I got tackled by a bloody mammoth dog, and at some point, between when I was fearing for my life and protecting my face from drool, I lost my bag." Nelson's voice increased in volume the longer he spoke, so by the time he finished his rant, he was yelling.

Slamming a fist on the steering wheel didn't ease Gord's frustrations one bit. That was a third of their score, gone. All the planning and expense they put into that store, there was no margin for error. His fury blinded him enough, he drove back toward town, determined to find out who that dog belonged to. Whoever that person was would pay for their dog's mistake.

Nelson patted himself down and made a second discovery, which he kept to himself. Somewhere along the way, he lost his cell phone. If Gord's tantrum was any indication, his temper was at its limit, so that bit of information would remain Nelson's secret.

ASSAULTING AN OFFICER

Constable Picault and his partner arrived at the scene of the crime eleven minutes after the alarm company notified them of a break in. Other officers were already clearing the scene, which left Picault to face Justin Peterson and his drooling dog, who were standing outside the front door of the jewellery store. Picault rubbed his temples after recalling his last interaction with the man—and the dog—and dreaded having to converse with him for one more moment.

"Mr. Peterson, care to explain what you're doing at the scene of a crime for a second time?" Picault did a visual inspection of the man wearing khaki pants and a black nylon jacket.

"Oh, hey there, Pee-cult. Karma and I are just doing our duty as citizens to keep an eye out for criminals."

"Mr. Peterson, it's our job to watch out for criminals. It's your job not to be one."

Justin sported a face-splitting smile as he lifted a small black duffel bag. "I think you're going to be happy Karma and I were here. Look what we found."

With a snap of his glove, Picault reached over, taking the bag from Justin. "What is this?"

"The bad guys must have dropped it."

Picault opened the zipper, and the contents sparkled under the dim streetlights. "Mr. Peterson, this is evidence in a crime. You shouldn't have touched it. I'm going to need you to show me where, and exactly how you found it."

"Oh, sure thing, Pee-cult." Justin spun and waved for Picault to follow him, who, in turn, waved along his partner. The three men and dog walked toward the back of the building where Justin showed them where the bag was found, underneath some shrubbery.

Picault asked him if it was hidden, like the criminals intended to come back for it, or out in the open. Justin explained that it appeared to be tossed there.

"Did you get a look at whoever did this? Their vehicle? How many of them were there? Anything?"

"No, sorry. Karma was too fast for me, and I thought they were robbing the bank across the street because..." Justin paused, looking uncertain. "That's where I'd go if I were a criminal. Easy money, you know?"

The tension in Picault's head was returning, so he ran his thumb and forefinger across his eyebrows, seeking the acupressure points to help alleviate headaches. "So you didn't see whoever did this because you thought they were robbing the bank?"

"Correct."

"Mr. Peterson, I am struggling to make sense of that. What were you doing out here at 2am, anyway?"

"Uh… well, Karma here likes to go for late-night jogs. She's a dedicated athlete."

Picault released a long exhale, unsure how to direct a line of questioning with a man who was one part deceitful, two parts stupid, and no parts tolerable. "What's the real reason you were here in the middle of the night, Mr. Peterson? I'm not interested in playing games."

The man's blue eyes flicked up to his left, and he shifted his weight from one foot to the other. "We were out for a stroll, then I heard the alarm, so I let her off her lea…" His eyes darted back and forth for a moment. "So, we… ah, shucks. I don't want to get in trouble, Pee-cult. You know I'm not cut out for prison life."

Picault's scowl was one part annoyance, two parts confused. He never liked fractions. "What are you trying to tell me?"

"I let Karma off her leash to go check out where the sound was coming from." Justin kicked a pebble on the ground, looking defeated.

As much as Picault wanted to toy with the man, making him feel as if letting his dog off her leash was a crime punishable by jail time—especially a dog who was a menace—he didn't have time for elaborate pranks. "Mr. Peterson, while letting your dog off leash to go seek out criminals is irresponsible, I'm not going to arrest you. But I'm not buying that you were exercising your dog. Why were you really here before you heard the alarm?"

The small man fumbled his words before he replied, "Okay. You got me. I was doing surveillance because last week when I was at the bookstore, I saw the men pull up and just sit in their van outside of the banks."

"You were at the bookstore? For... for comic books?" Picault wasn't sure which lie was more believable: the dog's midnight jogging habit, or Justin Peterson reading.

"I was buying a copy of *King Lear*, thank you very much. Shakespeare's *King Lear*. William Shakespeare, in case you didn't know."

"I'm familiar with Shakespeare; I just didn't know you were." With a shake of his head, Picault realized the conversation was veering so far off track, so he continued, "Back to the relevant information. You were in the bookstore? Which day?"

"Saturday; two weeks ago."

He jotted down the information. "Okay, Saturday. And why didn't you call the police when you saw this happen?"

"To report what? What would you have done if I said, 'Hey, there Pee-cult. I see two guys in a white van parked outside of the bank'?"

The man was right. At the very most, *if* a patrol car was available, they could have had someone swing by to check out a suspicious vehicle, but if they weren't doing anything wrong, there wouldn't be anything the police could do. Still, he didn't want to encourage vigilante idiots roaming town, causing more problems.

"I see your point. However, in the future, if you see something suspicious, please report it. We can't be everywhere at once, so we rely on community cooperation, but we don't want citizens putting themselves in harm's way."

"Aw shucks, Pee-cult. That's mighty kind of you to say so, but I've got Karma. She even found the jewellery, too."

"The dog found it?"

"She sure did. Come to think of it, you can talk with her about whatever the criminals looked like or what they drove. Pretty sure she tussled with them and that's why they dropped the bag."

Tension. Headache. Returning. "Mr. Peterson, I appreciate the offer, but I'm not the Dog Whisperer. I can't converse with your... your... creature."

"No, no. You don't whisper. She sends messages by blinking. Morse code or something. I'm not totally sure, but I blink back in case it's some secret message. Maybe you'll have better luck figuring it out."

Where are my painkillers? Picault stared down at the dog who was sitting beside her owner with a goofy grin, tongue lolled out to one side, and a string of drool connecting straight from her mouth, all the way to the small puddle in the dirt. *Morse code. This guy is something else.* Just for kicks, Picault blinked rapidly at the dog to see what happened, and before he could refocus his vision, he was on his back with the dog standing over his face. A new string of drool had connected to his left ear.

"Karma, no." Once Karma disengaged, Justin reached his hand down to help Picault up, which he refused. "I don't know what you said to her, but it must not have been very nice. She might not want to talk to you now."

"The feeling is mutual." Picault dusted himself off, mortified he let the dog get the better of him a second time, and infuriated he was stuck dealing with this buffoon again. "Is there anything *you can* tell me? Anything helpful?"

Justin pursed his lips as his eyes danced around, thinking far harder than his brain appeared capable of. He looked like a glitching robot. "They must have parked around back here. There were no cars out front."

Picault jotted down another note. "Okay, that's good. Thank you for that. Anything else?"

"They must have gone that way down the alley, because they didn't pass me, and I came from behind the politician's office."

"Okay, thank you. That gives us something to work with. We'll just hope other security cameras picked up something more useful."

92

"Listen… Do you need me for anything else? Cork…" Justin paused, his eyes flicking around again. "My wife is probably wondering what's taking me so long, and I can't tell her to put a cork in it."

"Just hang around for a few more minutes and I'll see if anyone else has any urgent questions. Otherwise, we have your contact information."

Justin bobbed his head in a repetitive nod with a stupid smile on his face matching his dog's. "That's pretty cool. I'm in the system now, I guess. You can call me anytime you want."

If there was any doubt about Mr. Peterson's guilt or innocence, he just provided the confirmation Picault needed. No one with a modicum of intelligence was excited to be in the police database. Especially not if they were guilty of a felony. Picault cut the man loose and got him out of the way so he and his colleagues could figure out what happened.

"You know what? Go ahead home, Mr. Peterson. I think we have everything we need here. Just promise me something."

"You got it."

"Don't stick your nose in any of this again. If I find you at another crime scene, I will arrest you for obstruction."

"Ah, come on now, Pee-cult. I thought we were friends. I was just trying to help."

"And as I said earlier, the way you help is by *not* being a criminal. Go home to your wife"—*the poor woman*—"and keep out of our way. We'll find these guys."

Justin hung his head, gave a defeated nod, then turned to walk toward the lone minivan parked down the street, with his dog following behind.

Picault stepped into the jewellery store for the first time, and he was shocked by the damage caused. Nearly all the display cases were cleaned out, except for the fake stuff. These guys knew exactly what to target. *Who are these thieves? And more importantly, how are we going to stop them?*

Fat Tony strolled down the street, hoping no one was watching him anymore. When he was far enough away, he whispered, "Corky? Where are you, man?"

A hand reached out from the alley between the bookstore and the politician's headquarters, right where Fat Tony left his friend more than an hour earlier.

"Geeze, man, I was getting worried. I tried to stay quiet so they wouldn't think I had anything to do with the heist. What happened over there?" A courageous man, Joshua Miller was not, but at least he wasn't in the police database in connection to grand larceny.

"I didn't see the guys at all, but Karma must have got to them. They left behind a bag of goods they tried to steal, so I turned it in. They asked me some questions and sent me on my way. These guys got away again, Corky. We've gotta get ahead of them somehow."

The name Corky was not growing on Josh, but he didn't bother arguing. "You're lucky they didn't think you were involved. This is the second time you've been around when these guys hit a mark."

"That's what Pee-cult said, but I think he knows I'm not a criminal mastermind."

Corky nodded emphatically. "Yeah, that's pretty clear."

"Thanks, man. I try to be a good person."

"Right. That's why." Josh declared it was time to go home, and shortly after, they returned Scarlett's minivan to its rightful place in the Peterson driveway and the Watchdogs parted ways for the evening.

As Justin crawled into bed for the night, Karma curled up on the floor beside him. Much to his surprise, Scarlett flung an arm over and pulled herself in to cuddle Justin's chest. In those moments, when she wasn't conscious or talking, she wasn't so bad. Even if her arm moving toward him made him flinch, once she was settled in, he made the most of it and appreciated a moment of peace between him and his wife.

Soon enough, the morning would come, and peace would be as fleeting as the sunrise.

Especially when she saw the condition of the inside of her minivan.

GRAND LARCENY

Picault, along with his fellow constables and Detective Staff Sergeant, worked through the night to piece together the scene of the latest crime. As frustrating as Mr. Peterson could be, he was the only reason they even knew what these criminals were driving. That's not much to go on, but it's more than they had before. Eyewitness accounts are notoriously unreliable, especially under duress, so having Justin confirm some of their earlier reports gave them a confidence boost. The man may not be smart, but he didn't seem to be rattled by much.

The crooks had been deemed "The Magic Men" by the Ontario Police because they had worked their way through several locations, never having been caught. They hadn't left a trace of evidence and never hit the same target twice. They had made a mockery of the police departments across the province, and Picault was determined to make sure his didn't suffer the same fate.

Once the sun rose, other businesses started opening. The immediate area surrounding the jewellery store was cordoned off, which drew the attention of early commuters and business owners.

Picault and his partner, a man by the name of Billings, took a tour of the street, asking all open businesses for their security footage from the night prior. Thankfully, everyone was eager to stop the criminals who had been terrorizing their town, so they handed over their footage without issue. Not having to stop to get warrants or subpoenas saved a lot of time and hassle.

The second last building on the street was the first of them all to have a hard-wired system, not operating on wireless internet. The Magic Men must have some sort of jamming device, which interfered with or stopped the wi-fi signal from functioning because every other business had grainy black and white static on their screen during the time of the robbery. This could be another break.

Picault and Billings watched the security tape thoroughly, analyzing the time, the direction The Magic Men were headed, and their vehicle. They learned nothing new from the information, but it corroborated Mr. Peterson's eyewitness account yet again.

After thanking the business owner, Picault and Billings returned to the scene of the crime with the one usable video feed, feeling defeated. They were hopeful that his co-workers had turned over something new in the past few hours.

As they neared the police tape marking off the back of the parking lot, a glint of something caught Picault's eye. He squatted down to look and found a glimmer of hope. A cell phone.

Picault snapped on a new glove and reached down to retrieve the device, but after repeatedly pressing buttons, the phone's screen remained black.

If they could retrieve any information from the phone, and assuming it belonged to one of the criminals and not a random patron walking through the alley, it could be a gold mine of information that could lead to the capture and arrests of The Magic Men.

The thought gave Picault a surge of adrenaline that a triple-shot espresso couldn't rival.

In order to ensure the chain of custody on the first real evidence the police had found, Picault spent hours taking photos, filing paperwork, and triple checking that every T was crossed. The phone got into the right hands that would have it examined in a tech lab within a few hours, though the results could take days to get back. Regardless, this could be a huge break in the case.

Nelson couldn't sleep the entire night. Gord's reaction to losing a third of their bounty meant they all had to suffer his incessant whining for hours upon returning home. One rhetorical question after the next, until his post-heist high wore off, and he fell asleep on the sofa.

The air mattress in the smallest of the three bedrooms had a slow leak, but being the third guy in the crew, Nelson always ended up with the worst accommodations. If Gord found out about his latest blunder, he knew he could be sleeping with the fishes, so a leaky air mattress still beat that.

It was also a better choice than a prison cot.

After a few hours of planning, Nelson came up with a solution, so Gord never had to know about his misstep. This was all that damn dog's fault. If she hadn't shown up, he would have been in the van, cruising for home with his loot and his cell phone.

First thing in the morning, Nelson left a note on the kitchen table saying he was going out for some supplies and would be back in a few hours. He just hoped Gord or Earle wouldn't be suspicious of him leaving a note rather than sending them a text.

He snuck out the front door, closing it quietly behind him so he wouldn't wake the oversized greying toddler on the sofa.

With the van headed due south, Nelson was convinced he could make this right and get back into Gord's good graces. Even if it came at great personal cost.

Rodney's Auto Shop was his first stop, so when Nelson parked, he stepped out to greet his old friend.

They ran together in a street crew back as teenagers, and neither of them had cleaned up their act ever since. Nor did they intend to. Crime pays.

"Rodney, my man. How are ya?"

"Well, if it isn't Smelly Nelly. What did I do to deserve your face showing up here?"

Nelson never liked that nickname. Especially coming from a man who wore the same navy-blue coveralls day in, day out, and hadn't brushed his teeth since before *The Rolling Stones* were able to collect a pension. His teeth were set so far apart, it looked like his tongue was in jail, and you could probably weaponize his stank breath. Even so, the man was the connection they needed, so Nelson played nice. "I need a new car, Rod. This one's been spotted, and we can't risk being seen in it again. You got anything that can fit a fifteen-foot-tall, miserable bastard?"

Rodney chuckled, throwing an oil-stained rag over his shoulder and wafting his halitosis toward Nelson. "I'm not sure. I've got a crew-cab pickup truck that might work. Everything else right now is small SUVs and compacts."

In the parking lot sat a black pickup truck that looked like it was in decent shape. Gord wouldn't be thrilled, but it would have to do.

"The good thing about this one is that it's the number one selling pickup in North America, and this is the most common colour. So if you want to blend in, it's as good as anything."

Music to Nelson's ears. "Sure. I'll take it. Just get it sorted for me and I'll be back in an hour or two with payment."

"You got it."

The next stop on Nelson's journey was the mobile phone store to replace what he lost. He hadn't quite worked out how to explain to Gord why he needed a new number, but he'd think of something. With a fake ID he'd used for the past few months, Nelson purchased a new phone, identical to the one he lost. After playing with it for a bit, he added any contacts he could remember—using his same code method, adding one to the last digit—downloaded a few apps he used previously, and customized the ringtone. He could finally breathe again.

Upon returning to Rodney's shop, the truck was ready to go with a clean VIN, fake insurance papers, and a phony plate. The van was nearly an even trade, so the new vehicle didn't end up costing as much as Nelson expected. Even better.

By noon, Nelson pulled back into the driveway of their secluded rental in their new truck. It might not take anyone off the line, but it had decent gas mileage, was roomy inside, and, like Rodney said, it blended in.

Gord was sitting having a late coffee after sleeping in. He was still furious over how last night went and made a personal vow to track down the small guy with the dog.

Once Nelson realized he lost his share of their score, Gord u-turned and headed back to the downtown core, parking in behind the businesses opposite the jewellery store. While standing in an alleyway far enough away where no one could see him, he spotted the offending dog. She sat beside a small man, looking proud of herself. When Gord watched the man hand Nelson's duffel bag over to the police officer, his temper almost got the better of him. It was enough of a risk going back to the scene just to find out about the dog. He knew going Hulk on everyone wouldn't solve any of their problems.

So, as he sat at the table the following day, flipping mindlessly through the newspaper, he was determined to track down that dog's owner and make him regret sticking his nose in their business. No one messed with Gordon Wright.

While blinded by rage, imagining himself dishing out revenge on the offending man and his dog, Gord neglected to read his text messages, so when a strange truck came tearing up the gravel driveway to their rental property, he went into commando-mode. He grabbed his gun from the kitchen counter and bolted out onto the rickety old porch in a t-shirt and his boxer shorts—thankfully not commando. If he were in Texas, the person would have been dead already, but Gord wasn't willing to risk anyone hearing a gunshot without just cause for shooting someone. They were secluded, but not far enough away from neighbours to have a shootout in peace.

As the truck approached, he saw a familiar face in the driver's seat and relaxed.

"Were you planning on shootin' me, Gordo?" Nelson climbed out of the driver's seat once he had the new vehicle parked.

"If you call me that again, I just might." The man's mood was clearly reflected in his facial expression. "What is this?"

"It's a truck." Nelson's smirk was not helping to keep Gord's volcanic temper from erupting.

"I can see that. Where's the van?"

"Well, I figured since we were already spotted, and then after last night, it was safer to ditch it. I went to Rodney's to get this. There's plenty of room for you."

Gord considered Nelson's decision for a moment before nodding and going back inside. Maybe that van was the source of their bad luck and without it, they could get back to what they did best. After they saw a man about a dog.

MISCHIEF

The eleven days following Karma's run in with the criminals were uneventful. There had been no new robberies, no potential sightings, and no literal or figurative alarms blaring. The Suburban Watchdogs were feeling pretty good about themselves, wondering if perhaps Karma had run them out of town. That wasn't the best-case scenario, because that left them to go terrorize somewhere else—the Watchdogs would have preferred to have them arrested—but at least they could rest easy feeling their families were safe.

Come Saturday afternoon, Justin had the weekend off, which meant he and Scarlett had been bickering all day. More so, she'd been yelling, and he'd been doing everything he could to avoid listening to her.

"Justin! Are you even listening to me? You can't let that dog up on the couch anymore. She's ruining it, and unless you want to spend another $3000 to replace it, you better keep her off."

In response to Scarlett's latest problem, which was number thirty-six for the day, Justin turned his back. That infuriated Scarlett even more until he started twerking.

"Stop that. I'm serious."

Justin didn't reply. He kept shaking his goods with such efficiency he could have made a mint from online tutorials. He definitely went to the wrong class at *Clippendale's*.

"What are you doing? I'm trying to have a serious conversation."

"And I'm trying to avoid one. Don't you ever want to have fun, Sweet Cheeks? You're too serious all the time."

Scarlett remained silent for a moment, then surprised Justin with a suggestion. "We should go out and have fun tonight. It might be good for us."

That statement stopped Justin's twerking abruptly, leaving him hunched over, hands on his knees, and his expression landing somewhere between confusion and constipation. "Go have fun? What about Ollie?"

"I'm sure one of the neighbours would watch him. I can ask Nicole or Anna if he can go over to one of their houses."

"Oh. Okay, then. As long as Ollie is okay with that, I could use some fun."

For the first time in a long time—months, at least—Justin saw his wife smile. She rushed off to make arrangements and get ready while Justin figured out a plan for the evening.

Hours later, Justin was dressed in his "fancy" jeans and a clean Henley shirt. He was at the bottom of the stairs when his wife descended, wearing a tight black dress with silver heels, and for a brief moment, he was reminded of the woman he fell in love with all those years ago.

"You look beautiful."

Scarlett's cheeks turned scarlet. "Thanks. You look nice."

Justin studied his wife's face for a moment, appreciating her beauty. Her hundred-dollar face cream had been doing its intended job. "Looks like you drew your eyebrows on a bit high."

Scarlett stared back at her husband.

"You shouldn't look so surprised." He handed her a light jacket from the front hall closet. "Anyway, if you get home before me, don't forget to leave the light on."

Scarlett's eyebrows drew up even higher. "What?"

"Don't forget to leave the light on. Karma and I are headed to Newmarket, and I don't know what time we'll be home."

"Justin, I thought we were going on a date!"

"Why would you think that? You said we should go have some fun."

After whipping on her coat, Scarlett grabbed her purse and stomped out the door in a huff. Justin was left standing in the foyer, confused for a beat before he shrugged his shoulders and brushed off his wife's reaction. In his mind, it was one of a hundred times that week she had been irrational.

"Come on, Karma. Let's get to the brewery and see if you can make any new dog friends."

Karma came trotting from the family room at the back of the house, pausing in the hallway to do a downward dog stretch.

"You're a natural yogi, Karm. Maybe I should ask Donna if you can teach a dog yoga class."

Justin clipped Karma's leash on her collar and grabbed the backpack with her necessary items for travelling: water bowl, treats, drool wipes, and so on. Then they were off to the nearby brewery for the monthly canine night.

An hour later, Justin was seated at a pub table with Karma cruising the room, sniffing her new friends. Justin watched each introduction with rapt interest, curious what dogs learned about each other that was so fascinating. He added a reminder in his phone to learn Morse code so he could find out from Karma.

A stocky man about Justin's height plopped himself in the open chair across the table. "Is that your Dogue de Bordeaux? She's a beauty."

"She is, but she's a French Mastiff. Not a Bordeaux, whatever."

"Dogue de Bordeaux is another name for a French Mastiff. Like how a Cane Corso is an Italian Mastiff, or a Boerboel is a South African Mastiff."

Justin stared at the man, deciding to dedicate his attention to this dog education he was receiving. "Wow. How'd you know all that?"

"I'm a vet."

"No kidding. In Newmarket?"

"In Alliston actually. I just like to bring my dog here when I can. She's over there with yours." The man pointed to where Karma was bouncing around with a pure white Dogo Argentino, who was near Karma in size, but taller and less bulky. "That's my Fluffy."

"Fluffy?"

The man released a booming laugh, drawing the attention of other patrons in the bar. "I know. It's a ridiculous name, but my daughter named her, and I didn't have the heart to tell her no."

"I can understand that. I have a boy at home who I'd do anything for. Ollie. We're from Alliston too."

"You're kidding? What are the chances? What's your name?"

"I don't know what the chances are, but I'm Justin Peterson. Pleasure to meet you, Doctor."

The man laughed again. "You don't need to call me Doctor. The name's Alvin Harper. Pleasure to meet you, as well." Alvin settled in with a beer in front of him, taking small sips in between speaking. "So where 'bouts in Alliston do you live?"

"The west end. The old subdivision."

"I know the area. We live on the outskirts of town, but my practice is on the main street."

Justin's face lit up hearing those words. "Did you see all the hoopla over the jewellery heist last week?"

Alvin shook his head, wearing a grimace as he placed his beer back down. "Sure did. Cops came and got my security tapes, which were useless static. Those criminals have all the businesses on the main street on high alert. Scary times."

Justin contemplated if he should tell Alvin about the Suburban Watchdogs and put the man's mind at ease, knowing they were on the case, but he decided against it. Better to keep things quiet, so no one ratted him out to Picault. He played it safe and didn't trust too easily. "I'm sure those guys will be caught in no time. Don't sweat it, Alvin."

"I sure hope so. My wife and I moved here from the city three years ago to get away from high crime rates. We wanted to raise our daughter somewhere safer, and lately, it's not feeling too safe."

Those words made Justin certain he and his friends were doing the right thing. They were not the only ones bothered by the crime spree ripping through their town. It was not only leaving people scared, but it was damaging businesses that hardworking people had dedicated their lives to.

"It looks like our dogs have become best friends," Alvin interrupted Justin's thoughts.

When he spun around, Justin found Fluffy and Karma cuddled together on the floor at the edge of the room. "Seems that way. Maybe we can meet up sometimes and let them play together."

"Ah, Fluffy would love that. She spends the day with me at the clinic, so she meets a lot of dogs, but I've never seen her take to another one like that."

"Karma only met other dogs at her yoga class, but they were all small enough to fit in her mouth. Plus, none of them came out of their purses."

That statement would probably confuse most people, but Alvin seemed to understand exactly what Justin was saying. He chuckled, spluttering some of his beer. "Dog yoga. That's a new one."

"Dogs *and* yoga, technically, but Karma is a natural." Justin paused for a second. "Hey, that reminds me, do you have any tips for bad gas?"

"For you or the dog?" Alvin's shoulders were shaking with breathy laughter.

"Karma. I love her to bits, but sometimes she's rancid. She smells worse than a Rafflesia Arnoldii."

Alvin's eyebrow raised in question. "A what?"

"Rafflesia Arnoldii? A stinking corpse lily?" Justin bobbled his head along with his explanation, as if it should have been obvious.

"Come by my clinic one day this week and I'll get her some probiotics. That might help."

"Thanks, Doc."

"My pleasure. Thanks for chatting with me, Justin, but Fluffy and I better get going. We'll see you one day this week. Whatever suits your schedule."

Justin and Alvin said their goodbyes, as did Fluffy and Karma. Once Justin finished his beer, he and Karma followed suit in heading home.

They arrived home to all the exterior and interior lights off and Scarlett's van parked in the middle of the driveway. Justin was forced to park his truck on the side of the road, but at least it was past the time of year when you'd get a ticket for it.

The pair unlocked the door, stumbled inside, and went directly to bed. The next day was bound to be another morning of dealing with Scarlett's fury.

UTTERING THREATS

Driving a pickup truck wasn't all that bad. It was easy to get in and out of for someone over seven feet tall, lots of legroom in the extended cab, and the gas mileage wasn't so bad. Nelson did all right. Make no mistake, Gord was still livid over him losing the merchandise from the jewellery store heist, but he had redeemed himself a little.

With the vehicle issue settled, it was time to make the little man and his dog pay for their interference. Nobody had the stones to stand up to the three-man crew before, and Gord was determined to retire with his legacy intact. They would not be taken down by a shrimp and his wrinkly dog.

The Magic Men had spent the last four days cruising the streets of Alliston, trying to spot the man. Gord knew it would be as difficult as spotting Earle's mom on a dairy farm, but they'd have to lie low for a while, so he figured they might as well use the time to dish out some retribution. With no heists possible for at least a few weeks, and knowing everyone was on high alert, they had to make use of their time somehow.

Cruising the streets of the small town was enough to make a grown man gag. The bucolic crescents, parents and kids skipping along together, people walking their beloved dogs—a bond Gord would never understand—and neighbours waving at each other as they went past. Gord didn't see the slightest appeal in living somewhere like that—where everyone had their noses in each other's business. That was why he and his guys were in their predicament in the first place. Small-town folks didn't know how to keep to themselves.

One way or another, they'd send a message that would have the entire town turning their backs because they'd be too scared to get in The Magic Men's way.

Scarlett was still steaming over the events of the past weekend. She couldn't believe Justin took that smelly, slobbering dog out for a date instead of her. It felt like her husband had another woman, but instead of a leggy blonde secretary, it was a stumpy, wrinkly canine with offensive breath and a gas leak.

Karma had been going to work with Justin most days because the guys in the office liked having her around for whatever reason—apparently dead fish breath is the way to those men's hearts, but they're plumbers so maybe their sense of smell was impaired. Today, however, she was at home. Justin had to do some work in a high-end home, and no one else would be available to keep Karma company at the office. God forbid the dog had to stay alone for a minute.

As Scarlett watched the dog's partially open eyes flicker back and forth while she yipped and barked in her sleep, she felt more resentful by the second. Things weren't great with her and Justin before the dog came around, but the past few months had been even worse, and her husband was oblivious to why Scarlett was so angry. She decided it was time to teach him a lesson.

"Karma." Scarlett clapped in Karma's face to wake her from her perch on the sofa. "Get up, you dumb dog."

Karma pulled her dangling tongue back in, making a repulsive smacking sound as she opened and closed her mouth, then dropped her front legs onto the floor. She walked herself out slowly until she was extended in a plank position, stretching with her back legs still on the sofa. Once she had achieved an optimal stretch, she released a loud fart that turned Scarlett's nose up in disgust.

"Ugh. You are nasty. I'll never understand what Justin sees in you." She clapped in Karma's face again. "Come on. It's time for you to leave. I've had enough of you." With a bit of coaxing, Scarlett got Karma to the front door, opened it, and shooed the dog outside. She was hopeful that with any luck, the dog would run away, never to be seen again.

Scarlett felt guilty for a fleeting moment because she knew how much her son loved the stupid dog too, but he was young; he'd get over it. She slammed the door shut, dusted off her hands after a job well done, and went to get the vacuum to clean all traces of the dog from her life.

Gord was pretty sure they'd covered 98% of the area in this blasted town with no signs of their offender. He was losing hope, but his rage had yet to be extinguished, pushing him to continue. The fire burning inside of him was too intense to let a few days of no results make him give up. There had been jobs he spent weeks casing before they got the final payout, and if this had to be the same way, so be it.

They turned onto a crescent in an older subdivision with cookie-cutter houses in various shades of orange brick. There were barely any trees lining the street because the houses were so crammed together, there wasn't enough room for foliage. The monotony of it all also made Gord want to gag. His life of crime had been exciting and fruitful, so he'd never have to live in a place where he couldn't recognize his own house after a few drinks.

They passed by a house with an old lady outside mowing her lawn, and Gord was impressed by her determination. She must have been in her 90s, with a hunched back and a head of curly white hair. Her skin looked weathered, as if she had spent a lot of time outside, but it was hard not to admire her work ethic; even for someone as cold-hearted as Gord.

Distracted by the old lady, all three men nearly missed the break they'd been waiting for. In front of a two-toned brick house with a minivan in the driveway sat a slobbery, wrinkly dog that was quite familiar.

They circled around the block so they could stop in front of the house, making their escape easier. Logic would have encouraged them to come back after dark, but with the dog out in the open and no threats around, the opportunity seemed too good to pass up. Most people were at work throughout the day and the old lady wouldn't be any trouble.

Gord instructed Earle to stay in the car behind the driver's seat while he and Nelson went to "deal with the dog." After that, they'd have no more interference. They were going to send a message loud and clear.

The stupid dog was wagging her tail as the men approached, with her tongue hanging out and shoestring drool dripping from her jowls.

The big man decided she had to be the worst guard dog in the history of time. When he was only a few feet away, just steps from the porch, Gord reached out his hand to charm the dog. "Hey there, girl. Who's a pretty doggy?" He continued walking forward with Nelson less than a metre behind him, and the dog didn't so much as budge, aside from her wagging tail. Gord placed one foot on the porch stairs, then another, and with no resistance, he was standing mere inches from the useless pooch.

Before he got an inch closer, the dog turned from Lassie to Cujo, bared her teeth, and started barking a loud, reverberating bark that could rattle the windows. She was relentless, with her dangling drool foaming and flinging several feet in each direction, despite Gord's hurried attempts to hush her. He discovered the dog wasn't going to be as easy to deal with as he thought. He spun on his heel to run back down the stairs, not realizing Nelson was right behind him. The smaller man landed on his back on the brick pathway as Gord plowed into him while running for cover. Gord muttered to himself, "This isn't the army." There was no honour among thieves, so no shame in leaving a man behind. Before he reached the end of the driveway, even with his long strides, the dog jumped on him, but thanks to his hulking size, she couldn't knock him down. Her relentless barking, however, was attracting far more attention than they needed.

Before Nelson even picked himself up off the ground, the front door of the house opened and a beautiful blonde woman sporting a scowl and yoga pants yelled, "Karma!"

Both escaping criminals took that to mean, "What goes around, comes around." As if this dog's interference was their comeuppance. Nelson took off running back to the truck.

Gord's temper rose, and vicious dog or not, he was going to make this chaos worth it. He turned to face the woman and shouted back, "Tell your little man to stay out of our business, or next time you won't be so lucky."

Scarlett was busy vacuuming inside, had music playing in the background, and was humming along while she worked to rid her house of all traces of that dog. She intended on pretending like that chapter of their lives never happened.

For the first time in months, Scarlett was at peace in her own home, feeling no remorse over sending Karma out to live a life on the streets. Just as the chorus of one of Scarlett's favourite songs came on— one she intended to belt out like she was auditioning for Simon Cowell—the dumb dog started barking on the porch.

Irritation was not the right word to explain how Scarlett was feeling. Pure, unadulterated rage coursed through her veins, and when the barking continued for several minutes, she decided to go tell the dog to keep quiet.

She opened the door and yelled, "Karma!" What she saw surprised her as Karma was racing down the driveway after an unnaturally tall man with hair the colour of their neighbour's orange-brick house. She was just about to fetch the dog when she spotted another man get up from the pathway in front of the porch and run toward a black pickup truck parked along the curb.

"Tell your little man to stay out of our business, or next time you won't be so lucky," the tall man warned. Then he pushed the dog off of him and jumped into the truck with the other man. A third man must have been in the driver's seat, because they peeled away in a hurry.

Scarlett stood, shaking on the front porch, as it dawned on her what had just happened. *Stupid Justin and his stupid street gang.*

After a few moments, while still in shock, June, from two doors down, came over to ask Scarlett if she was okay. The woman grew up in a crime-riddled area of the city, so things like this were nothing new to her. She would have whacked all three men with a shovel before they even had a chance to swipe her purse, then went and sat down for tea and crumpets.

Crime was something Scarlett had never come face-to-face with before, and this was too close to home in every sense, so her reaction was the complete opposite. If the dog hadn't driven them off, who knows what they would have done to her. Considering that was all she needed for tears to fall.

June sat in the wooden chair on the porch beside Scarlett and reached out to take her hand. "I pressed the emergency button on my Medic Alert. The police will be here in a moment."

A meek nod was all Scarlett could manage as she wiped the tears from her cheeks. Just to add insult to injury, Karma made her way onto the porch and rested her head on Scarlett's knees, looking up at her with sad eyes. For the first time in the several months since Justin brought Karma home, Scarlett patted her on the head. The dog's soft fur and dopey face helped to calm Scarlett's racing heart and steady her breathing.

An OPP cruiser pulled up in front of her house and two uniformed officers climbed out—one tall, lean man with umber skin and cropped black hair, and an average height curvy woman with a long brown ponytail and fair skin. They both look friendly, but most importantly, they made Scarlett feel safer.

INTIMIDATION

The male officer greeted Scarlett and June on the porch. "Good afternoon, miss. Did you call the police?" His subtle British accent was surprising, but it made him sound like a refined James Bond.

June spoke up, "I did, Constable. I live a few doors down, and I saw a commotion with some men who looked like trouble."

"Could you elaborate on that for us? Have the men left?" The man swiveled his head around while his thumbs were hooked on his belt loops. Hardly on high alert.

The glare emanating from June spoke volumes, and Scarlett suppressed a chuckle at the woman's bravery. Nothing fazed her.

"Of course they left. I'd have trimmed their hair with my lawnmower if they hadn't, and we wouldn't be sitting on the porch waiting for you. I'd be digging a hole in my garden." June's intensity startled both officers. Even Karma looked a bit concerned.

The pair of civil servants nodded and continued asking questions. Scarlett and June relayed their perception of events, though Scarlett neglected to mention that she had kicked the dog out of the house on purpose. She made it sound like the dog accidentally got outside, and she was unaware.

The situation had shed light on Justin's determination, and for the first time, Scarlett understood his desire to stop the criminals himself, rather than relying on the police. It's not that the police don't want to stop the bad guys, but they're forced to always play catch-up, reacting after a crime has taken place.

Well, Scarlett was not going to sit around and let those criminals push her around. No; she'd take a page from June's book and stand up for herself and her family. If those guys came back, they'd be sorry—which they should be because they lived in Canada.

When Justin got the call from Scarlett about what happened at the house, he was a combination of furious and nauseous. For a moment, he was worried about what could have happened and the dangers the ladies in his life faced, but he felt confident Karma could handle herself.

He left work seconds later and headed straight home.

As he was rounding the corner onto their crescent, he spotted the police car out front. He also wondered why Karma had been outside by herself and considered himself lucky that she didn't run away or get hurt. He added that question to his mental list of things to ask Scarlett.

The minivan was still parked in the middle of the driveway, so Justin stopped his truck in front of the old lady's house a few doors down and walked home to find June, Scarlett, Karma, and two police officers inside their living room. June and Scarlett were seated on the sofa, and the two members of the OPP were standing on opposite sides of the room.

"Mr. Peterson, I presume?" the female constable, Michaels, asked.

"I am; Justin. Do you know a Pee-cult?"

The woman raised her eyebrow. "A what?"

"Not a what. A who. Pee-cult," he enunciated.

"Do you mean Picault? René Picault?" the tall man asked with an accent that caught Justin by surprise.

Justin glanced at him, noticing his nametag. "Yeah, my buddy, René. We've met a few times. Is he working today, Lee… Lee-chester?"

The man's eyes darted around the room, wondering if the short guy was addressing him, but realized a botched attempt at his last name from years of mispronunciation. Leicester clarified, "It's pronounced Lester."

"You guys really should get that looked into. Whoever makes your nametags is lousy at spelling. Say, you're not Canadian, are you?"

"I am Canadian, Sir; I was just born elsewhere."

"Do you need a cuppa tea or something, Lee-chester?"

"I'm fine, thank you," the officer replied, blowing out his cheeks and crossing his arms.

Justin addressed his wife for the first time since entering the room three minutes earlier. "Are you okay, Sweet Cheeks? They didn't hurt you?"

Scarlett was surprised and touched by Justin's concern. She expected him to check on the dog first. "I'm fine. Just shaken up. They said next time I won't be so lucky if you don't stay out of their business."

Justin was perplexed—which wasn't new or unusual—because, as far as he knew, the bad guys had never seen him. The only way they could have made the connection was by Karma. "How did Karma get outside? I didn't think they'd ever seen me, so that's the only way they'd know… if they recognized Karm."

Suddenly, the tissue in Scarlett's hand appeared very interesting, and she avoided making eye contact with anyone. "I'm not sure how she got out."

"Did she learn to open the door? I know she's smart, but without thumbs, that would be hard for her." Justin kneeled down on the ground beside his beloved canine and she promptly licked his face. "How did you get outside, girl?"

Scarlett glared at the dog with a renewed hatred because she was receiving Justin's affection. So what if the dog saved her from being attacked in her home? She'd done nothing but upset their family dynamic since the moment she arrived, and Scarlett no longer felt any sympathy toward her for kicking her out.

"I'm going to have to check the fence in the back to see if she got out that way. I don't want her escaping again. She's my leading lady."

Those words added more fuel to Scarlett's fury and before she could extinguish it, she blurted out, "I let the damn dog out, Justin. I put her outside and hoped she'd run away because I'm sick of her. Sick of the attention you give her and how much Ollie loves her. I'm sick of her drool and hair all over the house. I'm angry that when I asked you to take me out, you took HER!"

Both police officers stood slack-jawed from their positions across the room. June was quietly sipping her tea, not batting an eye at the unfolding drama. Hearing her young neighbours bicker wasn't uncommon.

Justin, on the other hand, who didn't normally get rattled by much, was overcome by his own anger. "You put her outside? Alone?"

"I did. And I don't feel bad about it. I'm a beautiful woman, Justin, and most men would be happy to have me as their wife, but not you. You'd rather have that dopey… ugh… whatever that thing is! So sue me if I'm jealous of the attention you give her."

"Maybe I give her attention because she doesn't spend her entire life telling me everything I do wrong, or how I can never make enough money to make her happy. *Maybe* I give her attention because she likes me."

Constable Leicester cleared his throat in an effort to bring the couple's attention back to the other individuals in the room. "Mr. and Mrs. Peterson, I'm sorry to interrupt, but there are more important matters to attend to here. Do you mind if I ask some more questions?"

"I'm sorry. Are you referring to me or the *dog* as Mrs. Peterson? Because I'm not so sure anymore." Scarlett stomped off toward the kitchen, muttering obscenities under her breath.

"I wouldn't marry my dog. That's weird," Justin shouted after his wife. He then settled his eyes on Leicester. "Right? That's not a thing, is it?"

Leicester grumbled something to himself. "No, Sir. People don't marry dogs." He glanced over at his partner with pleading eyes.

"Mr. Peterson, if you don't mind, we have plenty of work to do, so if we could just ask you a few questions, we'll be on our way," the woman stated.

"Shoot." Justin's eyes popped wide open, and he threw his hands up in the air. "No, wait, don't shoot. I mean, ask the questions."

"Put your arms down, Mr. Peterson. No one is going to shoot you."

"Pee-cult said he was going to tase me for helping a guy, so I can't be too sure." He took a seat in a beige slipper chair set opposite the teal-coloured sofa, where June was still casually sipping her tea as if this was a normal afternoon of finger sandwiches and police interrogation. "Ask away, then."

For the next thirty minutes, the officers grilled Justin about his interactions with the criminals, and again took note of anything he may remember from prior encounters. Scarlett returned to the room to give another play-by-play of what happened an hour earlier, and despite her shaking hands, her fury never diminished.

Justin begged the police to do something, explaining that intimidation was a crime. Those men threatened his family, and if it weren't for Karma, there was no telling what they would have done. Sadly, the police were bound by the letter of the law and there was no arrestable crime. Since they didn't even know the men's names, a restraining order wasn't possible. The Petersons were left to fend for themselves.

"I'm sorry we can't be of more assistance, Mr. Peterson. I recommend keeping your eyes open for anything concerning and dial 911 if you feel threatened." Leicester tipped his head toward the Petersons. "Cheerio."

"Ah… and a Fruit Loop to you, good sir," Justin replied with a curtsy, tugging his imaginary skirt.

Leicester and Michaels left, and it was time for Ollie to come home from school, so Justin and Karma walked down to meet him and the neighbourhood kids to make sure they got home safely.

Ollie came running across the school yard when he spotted Justin and Karma, elated to see his furry friend and dad. "What are you doing here?"

After rustling Ollie's hair, Justin replied, "I wanted to come see my favourite son."

The other kids walked home together as per usual, with Justin, Ollie, and Karma walking behind. Justin's eyes were constantly scanning the area, looking for pickup trucks as Scarlett described the getaway vehicle, and for white vans just to be safe. Multiple vehicles weren't something Justin had considered before, and it appeared the criminals might be harder to catch than he initially thought.

But nobody was going to show up in Suburban Watchdog territory, threaten them, and get away with it. Not when Karma was ready to handle things.

HATE CRIME

When Morrie returned home after a long day at work chasing rodents and insects, he was surprised to see Justin's truck in front of the Peterson's house. Normally, Morrie was the first one home. He didn't think much of it, assuming Justin had a slow day and came home early, or possibly he was sick.

After greeting his children inside the house, Morrie's wife mentioned that there was some drama in the neighbourhood. According to June, who lived across the road from them, the police were called to the Peterson home.

Most of the neighbourhood was familiar with Scarlett's temper and Justin's... whatever you could call

Justin… so it was not a stretch to assume the woman finally snapped and assaulted her husband. Morrie was concerned for his friend, so he told Nicole he'd be back shortly. He was going over to check on Fat Tony.

As soon as Morrie opened the front door, there was Justin and Karma standing on the other side, looking no worse for the wear.

"Hey, Whitey. You got a sec?"

"Sure. But we have to take a walk because Nicole is allergic to dogs."

The men walked along the south side of the street, toward the main road their crescent branched off of. They were several hundred metres from home before Justin explained what happened earlier in the day. "Scarlett was jealous because I took Karma on a date, but it wasn't even a date because Karma just hung out with Fluffy the whole time while I talked to Dr. Alvin."

"Slow down a second." Morrie slowed his pace so he could process Justin's words. "I'm confused."

"What's confusing? Karma and I went to dog night at a craft brewery in Newmarket last Saturday. I met this guy named Alvin, who is a vet in town, and Karma snuggled up with his doggo somethin', Fluffy."

"Ohh-kay." Morrie still didn't understand how that explained anything but hoped it would make more sense as his friend continued. "Then what?"

"Scarlett was jealous because she wanted me to take her on a date. But how was I supposed to know? She said we should go out and have some fun. It never crossed my mind that would be something we'd do together."

Morrie sucked his top lip in between his teeth and clamped down on it to keep himself from saying anything he'd regret. "So you took your dog on a date."

"Not a date. That's weird. We just went out to meet some other dogs."

Karma continued pulling Justin down the street and, given that the man barely outweighed her frame of solid muscle, he didn't stand a chance of stopping her.

"So Scarlett was jealous and today, since I didn't take Karm to work with me… Woah girl. Slow down!" Justin jolted forward as Karma discovered a telephone pole to sniff in the distance and couldn't get there fast enough. "Good girl," he said as she finally slowed once she reached the pole, allowing Morrie to catch up. "So today, Scarlett kicked Karma out of the house because she was mad."

Morrie assumed that was the extent of the drama, and perhaps the dog was picked up by a by-law officer and brought home. "That was pretty cruel of her. I'm glad Karma made it back home safely."

"She never left. At least, I don't think she did. Scarlett said she just heard Karma barking like a mad woman, so she went outside to give her heck—which is ironic, considering how often she barks like a mad woman—and Karma was jumping on the tall guy. They found my house."

Those words caused Morrie's blood to run cold. "They found your house? How is that even possible, Justin? You said they'd never even seen you!" Morrie's voice was raising with each word because the terror he was feeling suppressed all rational thought.

"They didn't find the place because of me. They found Karma! If Scarlett hadn't put her outside, they never would have known where I lived. I'm sure of that, Whitey."

Words escaped Morrie's brain. He was stammering, not making any sense, trying to figure out what this meant. Finally, he was able to speak. "Did you call the police?"

"June did. She saw the guys take off. She knows how to spot trouble."

Maybe she's the real Watchdog of the neighbourhood, Morrie thought, *because she never misses a thing.* "What did the police say?"

"Nothing much. They can't do anything because no crime was committed. Told me to keep my eyes peeled."

"This is the opposite of what we were trying to do. I knew this was a bad idea. We wanted to protect our families from criminals in town, and now we've literally brought them to your home. We have to stop this before someone gets hurt."

Justin stopped walking… Well, he tried, but Karma didn't, so he stutter-stepped and carried on. "They would have no idea the rest of you exist, Whitey. Even if they did, they'd have no reason to assume we live on the same street. You and your family are totally safe. The only way we can keep mine safe now is to stop these guys. The cops can't do anything until a crime is committed, so we need to catch them in the act. We have to stop them *before* anything worse happens."

Morrie's first instinct was to argue, but he took a breath to calm himself and considered Justin's perspective. The man may be short, skinny, and dim-witted, but he didn't lack loyalty or bravery. If the roles were reversed and it was any of the other guys' families at risk, Justin would do anything to protect them. Morrie was as confident in Justin's loyalty as he was in Brendon's cheapness.

"Fine. We'll talk to the other guys and see how they feel about it, but this isn't a game anymore. First sign of trouble, we call the cops."

Justin returned Morrie's words with a nod and a smile, and Karma pulled him the rest of the way home. Dogs were always stronger in a pack.

Constable Picault arrived at work Tuesday evening to a bunch of clamouring in the break room. That's not unusual, but once he heard the name "Justin Peterson" mentioned, he groaned and walked into the room to find out what the irritating man had been up to.

"Hey, Pee-cult," Leicester shouted clear across the room.

His partner, Denise Michaels, slapped him on the shoulder. "Oh, hush, Lee-chester." Picault always had a feeling Denise had a crush on him, so when she jumped to his defence and blushed when he nodded his appreciation, that became more of a probability than a possibility. An idea he wasn't opposed to.

"I see you've met Mr. Peterson."

"Sure did. He says you two are friends now. He asked for you by name... Kind of." Leicester's head tipped downward, but his shaking shoulders could not hide his laughter.

"Friends is not the word I'd use. The man has grown on me like a hemorrhoid and he's twice as irritating."

The other officers in the room burst out laughing.

"So what has my new friend been up to in the"— Picault looked down at his watch—"fourteen hours I've been off?"

"Well, we suspect The Magic Men showed up at his house today. They threatened his wife."

Picault nearly dropped the cup of coffee he was pouring, crushing the paper cup in his hand while attempting to catch it. He grumbled as he swiped the front of his uniform with a stack of brown paper napkins, cursing Justin Peterson for ruining his day when he wasn't even around. "They showed up at his house? But he said they'd never seen him."

"That's what he says. He wasn't home at the time, but we figure they recognized the dog."

That damn dog. Picault asked for every detail regarding the encounter, and once he was satisfied he had milked Michaels and Leicester for every bit of information, he returned to the cluttered desk he shared with several other officers and started rummaging through paperwork. He made a note of the new vehicle The Magic Men were seen driving and any additional details, like physical descriptions of the two men Mrs. Peterson saw. It stung to admit, but as annoying as Justin was, he had provided the police with pertinent information they didn't have before.

Once he caught up on the administrative things, he shouted at Billings to meet him in the patrol car so they could hit the streets. Any smart criminal would steer clear of being spotted after a confrontation, so the chances of finding these guys doing anything shady were slim, but spending time searching beat sitting inside, filing paperwork, reading old reports, and waiting for action.

The night shift passed with only a few calls—one domestic "misunderstanding" that would require a follow up later in the week, one false alarm on a home invasion that turned out to be a raccoon, and one drunk driver, who received the full extent of Picault's pent up anger. He had no compassion for drunk drivers at the best of times, but with The Magic Men and Justin Peterson ratcheting up Picault's frustration level, he was happy to throw the book at the drunken idiot.

All in all, it was not a productive night, but in the world of policing, boredom was a good sign.

Perhaps The Magic Men also had enough of Justin Peterson and were packing up to leave town. As nice as that would be for the residents in the area, Picault had been champing at the bit to capture these guys—a task that every police precinct in the province had failed at. He wasn't just eager to catch them because of the promotion opportunities that would come along with it, but because he took his job seriously and valued his work.

His mother may call it a hero complex, but armchair psychologist's title or not, he wanted to protect the people he promised to. Begrudgingly, even Justin Peterson.

So, no. The Magic Men couldn't leave town. Not until they were leaving in a paddy wagon, wearing ankle chains.

ANIMAL CRUELTY

G ord was furious. That wasn't out of the ordinary for the hot-tempered man but being bested by that dumb dog for a second time enraged him. He wanted to send a message with violence. One that couldn't be ignored.

Most humans had a soft spot for animals, but Gord was not one of those people. He wouldn't have hesitated to teach that dog a lesson. Her interference in the jewellery store heist cost them at least twenty grand, and that was inexcusable.

He'd spent the last thirty-six hours replaying their encounter in his head, but instead of envisioning how it actually went, being run off by a wrinkly dog and a skinny woman in yoga pants, Gord imagined a very different scenario.

One in which everyone in Alliston would learn not to mess with Gordon Wright.

Earle interrupted Gord's thoughts by slamming a frying pan down on the stove in preparation to make fried eggs. The man had an affinity for eggs, which stunk up the entire house. If Gord wasn't so dependent on the man's—albeit subpar—alarm deactivating skills, he'd kick him out of the crew on the basis of his egg stink alone.

"Nelson has been acting strange the past few days," Gord confided in Earle. "Ever since the jewellery store heist, it seems like he's keeping a secret."

Earle shrugged his shoulders, indifferent to the observation. "Nelson is a weird cat. As angry as you are with him, though, he's just as mad at himself. Don't think you need to be tough on him to make him pay for the mistake. He tried to make amends by getting us a new whip, and he's still working at selling everything we got."

"Something still seems off. I can't put my finger on it, but between the two of us, we need to make sure he doesn't go anywhere alone."

Earle lifted his head to make eye contact with Gord, staring into the big man's angry eyes. "That bad? What are you thinking he's up to? Snitchin' or somethin'?"

"I'm not sure. I don't think that's it because he knows I'd kill him, but there's definitely something off about him."

Just then, Nelson walked into the kitchen to find Gord and Earle seated at the table. "I'm going to head down to the city to fence a few more items I have lined up. I'll stop in at Rodney's to see if we can get another vehicle, too."

Gord muttered a curse word, irritated that he had to get rid of the pickup truck already. It was his favourite vehicle to drive so far. "Earle will go with you in case you need backup."

Nelson furrowed his brows, looking at Gord. "I've never needed backup before. Earle could probably use the time to research the next alarm system he needs to disarm before we have a repeat performance."

The overall tension in the room was palpable at the mention of their last robbery. Heat crept up Gord's cheeks, but he reminded himself not to let on that he was suspicious of Nelson. "Just take him with ya. He's got plenty of time to figure out the alarm before our next job."

"Well, all right then. Let's get a move on. Criminals have schedules to keep."

Gord was surprised by how easily Nelson gave in to having Earle tag along, and that helped ease his mind.

The two men set off to sell some stolen jewellery and visit the man with the bad teeth for another vehicle. This town was costing more than they were making, and if the next job didn't go off without a hitch, they might have to delay their retirement plans.

That just wouldn't do.

Thursday evening, Justin decided it was time to stop in to see his new friend on his way home. Aside from Tuesday, when he was off work early, he hadn't had a chance to stop in, but it would be rude not to accept Alvin's invitation, and Karma's flatulence was getting out of control. Earlier that day, she nearly smoked out the office with her mustard gas. And that was a room full of plumbers who had gone nose-blind to foul odours.

Justin pulled into the parking lot behind the veterinary clinic, *Hooves & Paws*, and leashed Karma before walking to the front door. As soon as the door opened, Karma took off running, towing Justin until he let go. He was left standing in front of the receptionist with a dumb look on his face as Karma disappeared down a hallway blocked off with saloon-style doors.

A robust brunette from behind the reception desk cleared her throat, and Justin noticed her severe expression.

"Uh, sorry. She's excited to see Fluffy, I guess." He shrugged, trying to play off the intrusion.

The receptionist plastered on a smile, likely in an effort to maintain their facility's customer service reputation, and picked up the phone. Her husky voice announced over the intercom that there was a French mastiff on the loose.

It only took a few seconds before Alvin appeared with Karma's leash in hand. "Justin, how are you?" Alvin didn't seem irritated by Karma's boldness, and simply handed the leash back to Justin.

"Good, Alvin. Sorry about Karma, here. She was excited to see Fluffy."

"Come with me and I'll grant her wish. Fluffy will be happy to see her, too."

Justin followed the portly man through a narrow hallway with several closed doors on either side. He reached the door at the end of the hall, which he opened to reveal a good-sized office. Fluffy's tail was thumping against the brown leather sofa she was curled up on, but as soon as she spotted Karma, she hopped down so they could dance around each other.

The sight made Justin smile, seeing how happy Karma was to be reunited with her new friend. Especially after the trauma she faced days earlier. "Would ya look at that? Like long-lost sisters."

Alvin chuckled. "It's good for dogs to be around others their size. They learn a lot from each other."

"Can Fluffy teach Karma to stop jumping up on people, because she won't listen to me?"

Gesturing for Justin to sit on the sofa, Alvin took a seat behind his large walnut desk and poured two glasses of scotch after getting a nod of approval from Justin. "You'd be surprised. Often, well-trained dogs will teach others how to behave, so you never know. Just like with kids, their friends rub off on them one way or another."

Justin considered getting a second dog for a moment, but quickly dismissed the idea, fearing that he'd end up in the pound himself. "I'm not keeping you from anything, am I? We just wanted to stop in and say hi."

"Oh, nonsense. No. You got here just as I finished up my last patient."

"How's that for timing?" Justin chuckled and took a sip of his scotch. "So, what's exciting in the life of Doctor Alvin Harper?"

Alvin's round stomach bounced as he snickered at his new friend. "Nothing much, I'm afraid. I spend my days working, and my evenings with the family. Brewery nights are the one night a month I go out. Basically, this clinic is my life, aside from my wife and daughter." He tilted his tumbler to his lips, taking a healthy swig. "How about Mr. Justin Peterson?"

Justin again considered telling Alvin about his true passion as a Suburban Watchdog but didn't want to bring attention to his neighbours after the events from earlier in the week. He opted for ambiguity. "Oh, you know. A little of this. A little of that. Spend as much time with Karma and Ollie as I can."

"Do you have a missus at home?"

"I do—Scarlett—but she doesn't like me much anymore. Can't ever do anything right in her eyes."

Alvin set his drink on his desk and leaned forward. "I'm sorry to hear that. Pardon me for the intrusion, and I apologize if I'm overstepping, but in my experience, the only way to fix that is by communicating with each other. Have you tried talking to her?"

"Every time I try, she just yells. I haven't lived up to her expectations, so she never lets me forget it." Justin stared down at Karma, watching her enjoy Fluffy's company. Her innocent happiness made him happy. If only Scarlett could find joy in the simple things in life. "I spent years really trying. I worked hard, went through an apprenticeship to get a decent job. Nothing is ever enough."

"My wife and I went through a rough patch about ten years ago. I thought I was doing the right thing by working hard to provide for us. She always wanted to stay home with our daughter, and I wanted to make that happen. But somewhere along the line, that wasn't enough for her, and she started to resent me for having a life outside of our home, even if it was just for work. It took a while for us to strike a balance." Alvin steadied his gaze on Justin. "I don't know if Scarlett has a life other than being a mom and wife, but perhaps that's part of her struggle. It might not be you she's angry with at all. It might be a lack of fulfilment."

Justin contemplated Alvin's words. "Less time earnin' a dollar, more time on the shot-caller, eh?"

Alvin let out a hardy laugh. "That's a good way to put it."

The two men talked for some time about their childhood and where they grew up. Alvin was a decade older than Justin but was raised only thirty minutes away. As they fell into a comfortable silence, the sound of air releasing caught both of their attention. Karma looked up at Justin with a satisfied expression.

"Al, we better open a win—" Before he could finish his thought, the stink hit him with an overwhelming force. He pulled his flannel work shirt up over his nose, seeking relief. Even body odour from a day at work was a welcome reprieve.

Alvin sat at his desk, fanning his face, laughing. "You're right. That is pretty foul." He leaned down, pulled open a drawer of his desk and grabbed a small box. "Here are some probiotics to try. They're in individual portions, so she gets two a day. If you can swing it, divide up her meals into three or four for now. If this doesn't help, I'll try to find a new food for her."

"Thanks, Al," Justin muttered from inside his shirt, refusing to risk a breath of Karma's putrid aroma. He stood to grab the box from Alvin. "How much do I owe ya?"

"Nonsense. On the house. You can come back next week, and I'll see how she's doing."

Justin smiled, pleased to have made a new friend who enjoyed his company. Something a lot of people overlooked about Justin Peterson, because they saw him as a stooge, was that he was unfailingly loyal. Just like man's best friend.

Thursday night, when Picault returned to work, he was thrilled to find the report from the tech department in his inbox. The Detective Staff Sergeant had already scoured the information, attempted to call and track the numbers in the phone's address book, but everything was cryptic. There was no discernible rhyme or reason to the information collected. As if everything had been input in some kind of code.

It seemed the missing cell phone was a dead end, without even so much as one picture. The only thing that might be helpful was a list of dates in the notes. The past dates were the days the previous robberies had happened. The electronics and furniture stores in February, the pharmacy in March, and the jewellery store in April. There were only two more dates listed, one in May and another in June. There was no indication what the targets would be, and it was likely as soon as they realized their phone was missing, they'd alter their plans, but this still told Picault he had two more chances to nail those guys.

And that was exactly what he intended to do.

FALSE PRETENSES

The week after the near confrontation with Scarlett and the brazen criminals, Morrie was still sick with worry over what could have happened. He wanted to keep his family safe just as much as the other Watchdogs, but he feared they'd put their families more at risk by painting a target on their backs. The criminals knew where Justin lived, and though they probably wouldn't assume the guys were neighbours, and Justin was likely the only one they knew about, one more failed interaction could mean bad news for the rest of them.

Despite the conversation Morrie and Justin had the week before, Morrie was unable to rationalize putting his family at further risk.

After deciding what he felt was best, he informed his wife he was going out for a few moments and walked across the street, passing June with a wave. She grumbled something in his direction, but he wasn't stopping to discuss neighbourhood gossip with the woman. She'd complain for thirty minutes about noisy kids and neglected gardens, which Morrie didn't have any opinion on. What others chose to put or not put in their gardens was none of his concern.

He brought his hand up to knock on the Peterson's white door with a patterned window, but barking on the other side alerted the homeowners to his presence. Apparently, Karma could be a decent guard dog. At least she sounded intimidating.

The door swung open, and on the other side was Justin, wearing a ruffled yellow apron and purple rubber gloves with bedazzled cuffs. Karma greeted Morrie by planting each of her front paws on his chest and hopping on her back legs to kiss his face. It was an impressive feat, given his height.

"Hey, Karma." He gave her a scratch behind the ear, trying to keep her tongue off of his. "I see the training is going well," he directed to Justin.

"She didn't knock you over. She's learning to be gentle."

Morrie chuckled at Justin's 'proud-dad' interpretation of Karma's greeting. Once he dislodged the dog and her four paws were back on the ground,

Morrie took in Justin's unusual outfit. "That's some getup you have there, Fat Tony."

"I'm a maid man." He laughed while performing jazz hands. "Get it? A made man?"

Morrie chuckled again, but quickly turned serious. "Yeah, man. That's kind of why I'm here. Can you talk real quick?"

"I don't think I'd make it as an auctioneer, but I can get going at a steady clip if you give me a second."

It took Morrie a moment to figure out Justin's reply before shaking his head and rephrasing his question. "No, I mean, do you have a minute to talk?"

"Oh, yeah, sure. I was just cleaning up Karma's hair while Scarlett and Ollie are out because Scarlett was having a conniption fit. You'd think after the dog saved her life, she'd be more grateful."

Wow. Conniption was a big word for Justin, and he used it properly. Morrie was impressed by his friend's expanding vocabulary. That didn't quell the nausea pooling in his stomach over the reality that Scarlett's life really was in danger because of their misguided attempts to keep their families safe. He couldn't imagine how scared Scarlett must have been, and it made a chill run down his spine, thinking if it had been Nicole.

"Well, that's why I'm here. To talk about what happened."

Justin raised an arm, directing Morrie into his family room at the back of the house. The light grey sectional sofa was immaculate except for one cushion, which was marred with dog hair and slobber stains.

"Don't sit in Karma's spot there. I haven't vacuumed it yet because she likes it a certain way."

A glance at his friend had Morrie wondering if Justin really thought anyone would choose to sit there, but he shook the question from his head. There was no point in trying to figure out what went on in that man's mind. Morrie sat in the corner opposite Karma's cesspool, where she promptly climbed up and spun in several circles, pawing at the cushion to fluff it up before she settled. Justin brought over a fleece blanket, covering the dog, and ensuring she was tucked in, then kissed her big, slobbery head. It was no mystery why Scarlett was put off by the dog's presence.

Justin moved to sit in a floral armchair opposite Morrie, angled beside the propane fireplace. He barely hit the cushion before he jumped back up. "Where are my manners? Can I get you something to drink? Do you want a sandwich or something? I think we have some apples." He was speaking to Morrie, but his eyes were directed at the ceiling, as if he were recalling the fridge contents from memory.

"Uh... no thanks, man."

Justin lowered himself back into the chair and nodded.

"So, I've been thinking about what happened the other day, and—"

"The playoff game? That was such a bogus call. I can't believe the ref could be so blind."

Ugh. This is going to take longer than I thought. Pushup. "No, about the bad guys finding out where you live; about them coming here and putting your family in danger."

"Oh, that! Yeah, those rat bastards gave Scarlett a good scare, but if she hadn't kicked Karma outside, they never would have spotted us. She's just lucky Karma didn't hold a grudge." Justin leaned back in the chair, his arms crossed over his chest, and an expression displaying righteous indignation on his face.

"Justin, that's not the point. You can't blame Scarlett for being angry with the dog, or for them tracking us down. Obviously, these guys aren't small-time crooks. They'd have found us sooner or later."

"I doubt it. They're wise guys. If they were smart, they never would have walked into Suburban Watchdog territory."

Morrie released a sigh, understanding that Justin didn't see the potential consequences of the criminals knowing where they lived. Who knew how far these guys would go. Maybe they'd resort to kidnapping or worse. That wasn't a risk Morrie was willing to take. "We have to stop this before things get out of hand. We can't put our families at risk anymore."

"You're darn right we do."

Justin's agreement took Morrie by surprise. "Um… Good. I'm glad we agree on that. I'd do anything to keep Nicole and my kids safe, so if this is the way things have to be, then I'm all right with that."

"I'm happy to hear that, Whitey. The reason this all started was because we wanted to keep our kids safe."

The conversation had gone far better than Morrie expected once he made his point. He expected arguing and resisting, assuming Justin wouldn't see another perspective, but he was being rational. "Thanks. At the end of the day, family is all that matters." Morrie smiled at the man, who continued to shock him. "Well, I'll let you get back to your housework before Scarlett gets back." Dealing with Scarlett's wrath didn't appeal to Morrie in the least. He might have sympathized with the woman at times, but he did with Justin too.

"Thanks for stopping by, Whitey. I'll see you at Corky's on Friday."

"Sure thing. Bye, Karma." Morrie looked at the dog, who was sleeping with her tongue dangling out to one side and her eyes open a sliver, rolled back in her head, displaying a slit of white. How a creature could be so ugly they were cute was a mystery.

Upon returning home, Morrie relayed to Nicole the conversation he'd had with Justin, and how understanding he was. They were both surprised by how easily Justin conceded and assumed the confrontation with his wife and the criminals knocked some sense into him. As if that were possible.

Nicole was never crazy about the vigilante mission to begin with, but she knew her husband wasn't a stupid man, and he would set limits when needed. That unwavering faith in him had never steered them wrong in the twelve years they'd been married.

As a family, they settled in for their weekly movie night after the kids finished their homework, and for the first time in weeks—maybe months—Morrie felt like he could breathe.

Justin returned to work cleaning the house after Morrie left, and he was pleased with how eager his friend was to ramp up their efforts. After the bad guys stormed Justin's castle, an eagerness sparked in him that renewed his determination to stop them. He was fortunate his fire-breathing dragon was there to protect his princess—even if she was more of an evil queen and could have stopped the bad guys in their tracks with one of her infamous tongue lashings.

Regardless, they were fortunate nothing bad happened—aside from Scarlett shouting at Justin for two hours straight after June left. That was nothing new, though. He considered for a second if he should have taken her on a date instead of taking Karma to the brewery, but all things considered, everything turned out better than a night out with his nagging wife. He met his new friend Alvin, and Karma met Fluffy. Plus, Karma got some probiotics, which were helping with her rancid gas. That alone was worth the risk of criminals appearing at their home, because the way things had been going, they were more liable to die from asphyxiation due to dog farts.

Nobody wanted that.

BRIBERY

J osh's wife, Lily, was still shaken up by the visit from the town's elusive criminals and asked if the men would have their guys' night elsewhere for the time being. Rather than cancel, they agreed to meet up at a restaurant on the main street, hoping with any luck they'd get a good meal, some laughs, and spot a black truck driven by a behemoth or one of his friends as described by Scarlett and Justin.

Morrie drove the four men in his wife's SUV so the other guys could have a drink if they wished, but they wouldn't be too far from home to walk if he chose to join them. They pulled into a parking spot lining the main street, about 100 yards from the restaurant of choice.

They walked inside while talking amongst themselves and were greeted by a petite hostess with bright blue hair and fair skin, displaying the tattoos she had creeping up her neck from under her mandarin collar.

"Good evening, gentlemen. Do you have reservations?"

Morrie opened his mouth to speak, but he was beaten to it by Justin. "Yeah, it looks a bit sketchy in here, but we're hungry, so we'll eat here anyway."

The short woman stared at the blond man, who was barely a few inches taller than her, with a dark brown eyebrow inching closer to her blue hairline.

"We don't have a reservation, or any reservations," Morrie clarified while giving Justin a stern look—which was disregarded.

"Ohh-kay. If you can follow me, I'll get you a table."

They trailed behind the woman, who seated them at a six-person table and placed menus in front of each of them, then disappeared.

"Hello, gentlemen. I'm Kayla, and I'll be your server tonight. Can I start you off with drinks?" Another colourful-haired petite woman stood at the head of the table eyeing the men—this one with purple hair, and Morrie wondered to himself if the staff was required to dress like the cast of *My Little Pony* or if they were just embracing their own uniqueness in the same way.

The men went around the table, each ordering a stiff drink—even Morrie. He figured if he only had one, he'd be fine to drive home when the time came. Kayla arrived back moments later, passing the drinks to each of them and asked if they were ready to order.

Josh started by ordering a chicken and shrimp entrée; Brendon requested a sirloin burger with fries, while Morrie opted for a pasta dish.

"Can I get the rib-eye, please, miss?" Justin added from behind his menu.

"Okay. How do you like your steak?"

Justin spun in his chair to face Kayla, dropping the plastic-encased menu onto his lap. "I don't know. I haven't tried it yet."

She seemed confused for a second but caught on quickly and didn't let the slightest hint of irritation show. "No, I mean, how do you want it cooked? Rare? Medium?"

"Oh, my apologies, miss. As long as it's not breathing no more, I'll let the chef decide."

With a tight-lipped nod, Kayla collected the menus and marched toward the computer to place the men's orders.

The short while before the food arrived had the men chatting about their next steps for finding the mysterious bandits.

"I don't know what we should do next. There's no point in us staking out the main street again, because for all we know, they could have left town by now. Plus, Lily was really shaken up over what happened with Scarlett."

"Anna was worried about it too. She wanted me to put in an alarm system, but no way am I paying for that," Brendon replied.

"I thought we were finished with this nonsense. There's no reason for us to put our families at risk trying to catch these guys. Justin and I already talked about this." Morrie agreed to form the Suburban Watchdogs because he wanted to protect his friends from their own stupidity, but his priority would always be the safety of his wife and children.

"What are you talking about, Whitey? I thought you said we had to stop this before it got out of hand!" Justin's outrage was obvious on his face as he clenched his partially full whisky tumbler.

"That is what I said. Stop this"—he waved his pointer finger around the group of men—"before someone gets hurt. Not stop them!"

Justin shook his head. "I'm disappointed in you. I didn't take you for a yellow-livered pansy. First sign of trouble and you're flaking on your friends. On your town." He pounded his fist on the table, rattling the silverware and startling other diners enjoying an otherwise peaceful meal.

"Woah, man. I thought we agreed. This has gotten too dangerous."

"I'm ashamed of you, *Morrie*."

The name Whitey had irked Morrie, but, for some reason, having Justin revert to his preferred nickname stung a little. "We can still keep our eyes out for them, Fat Tony, but I'm not putting my wife or kids in danger. That's what scares me more than anything."

"Me too, man. You don't think those guys showing up and almost hurting my wife scared me? Hell yes, it did. But that means they need to be stopped. So, with or without you, I'm going to do it."

Morrie considered Justin's words and understood that the best way to keep him safe was to have his back. If he was determined enough to go after the criminals by himself, he could really be in danger. He wasn't thrilled about it, but Morrie conceded. "Fine. We'll make a plan to track these guys down, but we're not confronting them. Understood? Like I said before, we call the cops."

Justin didn't respond. He only smiled as Kayla delivered their meals.

Justin was the last to finish eating, but the small man barely consumed half of his meal. The other men cleaned their plates without hesitation, so when Kayla returned, she asked Justin, "Do you wanna box for that?"

He tilted his head to look at the purple-haired server, appearing deep in thought. "By all means, you can keep it. I could never hit a lady."

The poor girl was confused, but she wasn't alone in that feeling. Without seeking clarification, she scooped up Justin's plate and walked away.

She's a quick learner, Morrie thought. "What are you talking about? Hit a lady?" he asked, rubbing his hands over his whiskered face.

"She asked if I wanted to box for it. No way, man. Maybe if she wanted to have a break-dance battle or something, I would have considered it, but I can't punch her."

Morrie's elbow was on the table and his fingers pressed into the bridge of his nose. With his eyes closed, he slid his hand up his forehead and into his hairline before he addressed Justin. "Not want *to* box, Justin. Want *a* box? Like a doggy bag."

"Ohh. That makes more sense. You're probably right." Justin glanced back over his shoulder, as if he hoped to catch Kayla in time to remedy his mistake. She was out of sight, so he didn't make any further effort.

The three other men at the table grumbled to themselves as they placed cash down to cover their cheque. Morrie stopped at the hostess station to drop a tip for the blue-haired girl as well, then they exited the restaurant.

With nothing pressing to rush home for, the men agreed to drive around the area for a while to see if they spotted the bandit's vehicle. For over two hours, the men wove up and down country roads, through town streets, and past small businesses that could be potential targets.

Nothing. Well, not nothing. Tons of black trucks, but nothing that appeared criminal.

The Watchdogs were left chasing their tails. The only option was to wait for the wise guys to rear their dastardly heads and stay ready to handle them like a game of whack-a-mole.

DRUG POSSESSION

After the less-than-stellar score from the jewellery store last month, Gord and his nefarious friends were poised to hit their next target and make up for lost profits. Given that their last efforts were foiled by a dog, that made the target all-the-more satisfying.

It was late in the evening, and such was small-town life, most businesses were closed for the day; at least the small businesses lining the main street, anyway. That was all that mattered. Breaking in during the middle of the night would have been highly suspicious, but not every target was suitable to break into during office hours. It took a lot of skill and recon to determine the best course of action. Gord was proud of himself for developing that skill over a lifetime of crime.

"Get in, get what we came for, and get out. No funny business." Gord pulled his ski mask down over his face, though if Earle did his job right this time, the security cameras in the area should have been rendered useless. Still, better safe than sorry. They learned that the hard way last time.

"Yeah, yeah. We know the drill. I'll give the signal when I have the alarm deactivated." Earle hopped out of the passenger seat and scanned his surroundings before proceeding across the empty parking lot.

A few minutes later, he was flashing the predetermined hand signal at his mates to let them know the coast was clear. The big man and Nelson disembarked, striding across the gravel to join Earle.

For Gord, picking a lock was child's play, so within seconds, the three men were headed inside the building. Unlike most of their targets, none of them had ever been in the back of this one, so they were going in blind. With headlamps shining light on the space, they made their best educated guess which rooms to hit first.

Decades of crime had paid off, because the first lock they picked led to exactly what they were looking for. A few swipes of their arms and their duffel bags were loaded with loot, sure to fetch a pretty penny on the black market.

They opened two more doors before finding an office, where they found some cash and other valuable goods.

With no interference, the men were headed out the way they had come in; not a single soul was any wiser about their activities. That was exactly how it was meant to happen. The small man must have gotten the message to stay out of their business.

Gord jumped in the driver's seat of their new vehicle and breathed a sigh of relief that his crew was back at the top of their game. A feeling of redemption washed over him as he drove off into the darkness.

No stupid dog was going to stop them.

Maybe retirement would happen as planned. More importantly, his reputation was still intact. He hadn't lost his touch after all.

Constables Picault and Billings were on patrol in Alliston when they received a call from dispatch about some suspicious activity downtown. They were only a mile away, stopping for a break at the only twenty-four-hour coffee shop in town, so they grabbed their takeout cups and headed in the direction of the complaint.

The caller dialled the direct number for the police rather than 911, unsure if it was an emergency, so there was no need to turn on sirens and make a ruckus through town. If something was fishy, it was better to arrive covertly, anyway. They started by driving around the front of the business in question, but upon slowing, they didn't notice anything out of the ordinary.

There was a security light on inside, but that was no different from any other night, as some stupid law makes it necessary to leave a light on in case of a break in so you can't be held liable if a criminal hurt themselves. Picault was always of the mindset that if someone broke in where they weren't supposed to be and injured themselves, it served them right. How anyone decided that was the fault of the property owner baffled him, but his job was to uphold laws, not write them.

Regardless, there were no movements inside, no broken windows, no alarms. The two officers agreed to drive around back so they could get out to investigate on foot.

When they arrived behind the building, they parked at a nearby salon, notified dispatch of their location and intentions, then exited the vehicle to inspect the area.

Just when they thought there had been a false alarm, Picault pulled on the door of the building, and it opened easily. He signalled to Billings to join him as he entered the space, gun and flashlight drawn. Methodically working their way through the hallway, they found most doors locked, except three. The last open door belonged to a near-empty stock room.

The Magic Men had struck again.

Sometime later, Picault and Billings were joined by their Detective Staff Sergeant and a litany of other OPP members combing the area for clues. Picault knew the men had two more planned robberies in the area after the cell phone discovery at the jewellery store, so he was furious that it was knocked down to one. The men struck their target earlier than he expected. He should have known because their MO all along was to keep everyone guessing. They obviously put a lot of planning into making sure no one else could anticipate when or where they'd strike next.

"The owner is on his way here now so he can get us a stock list and we can figure out what these guys took," Picault relayed to the detective in charge after calling the listed property owner.

"Thanks. I'm getting sick of these guys." Detective Staff Sergeant Chen shook his head, his lips set in a tight line. He'd been working hard on this case since the first break in at *The Gadget Factory* more than three months earlier. He'd aged tremendously in that time.

Everyone on the force wanted to stop these guys, but with each passing day, it felt more hopeless.

"You and me both. They're always two steps ahead."

When a middle-aged stocky man arrived and provided ID to get past the officers patrolling the perimeter, he introduced himself to Detective Staff Sergeant Chen and Constable Picault. "Good... uhh... I guess, good morning, gentlemen. I'm Alvin Harper."

Picault reached out to shake the man's hand. "Sorry to disturb you, Dr. Harper, and to meet under these circumstances."

Alvin nodded at Picault but seemed more bothered by the condition of his clinic than being roused from bed in the middle of the night. "I appreciate you calling. What do you need from me?"

The detective took a step forward to address Dr. Harper. "If you could find an updated stock list, we'll start comparing what you have to determine what's missing. Also, if you can take a look around to see if anything is out of place and help one of our constables retrieve your security footage for the last few hours, that would be great."

"Sure thing. Whatever you need." Alvin turned toward the nearby reception area and planted himself in a black leather computer chair behind a tall birch-veneer desk.

Picault took some time to study the lobby area of the clinic, noting the camera placements, security system stickers on the windows, and other clues that would have given criminals some insight into the facility.

A few minutes of clacking on the keyboard and the printer roared to life, shooting out a four-page list of inventory. "Here you are, Constable."

"Thank you, Sir." Picault retrieved the papers from Alvin. "Could we retrieve that security footage?"

"Of course." Alvin trudged his way to his office, where he saw the damage done for the first time. They had ransacked his filing cabinet and desk drawers. "I had our petty cash in my desk, so I'm assuming they got that." Alvin's face paled. "And my prescription pads."

Picault understood the significance of that. With a doctor's official prescription pad, it was easy for criminals to prescribe themselves whatever pharmaceuticals they wanted. "I'm sorry, Dr. Harper. We're doing everything we can to catch these guys."

Alvin nodded with a grim smile, rifled through some files amongst the chaos, and handed a manila folder to Picault. "Here. Those are the codes and account information for the security company. A lot of good it did me." The stout man dropped his chin and ambled out of the room on the verge of tears.

Picault was feeling gutted for the good doctor. Each time he responded to a call for a break and enter, it was never easy. While some people overlook the trauma that it can cause, assuming because it's not a violent crime, it's only material things at stake, but that's not true. Picault had witnessed hundreds of people over the years struggle to return to a sense of peace and security in their own home or business. The Magic Men were violating the people of his good town in an unforgivable way. With renewed determination, he walked back toward the stock room to begin the tedious task of matching supplies with the list.

At some point, in the hours Picault was creating a master list of what was stolen, Detective Staff Sergeant

Chen excused Dr. Harper with the understanding he could be reached by telephone or come back should they need him. When Picault exited the small, sterile stock room with his newly compiled list, he tracked down the detective to explain what he had discovered.

He tucked his pen into his breast pocket and relayed the pertinent information. "So, they took a few vials of Pentobarbital, Metacam, and Amoxicillin. It looks like they stole the entire stock of Ketamine, Acepromazine, Propofol, Clavamox, Diazepam, and Oxytocin. They snatched a few prescription pads, some sterile scalpels, scissors, and gauze, and from what Dr. Harper said, about $1200 in cash."

The detective stared at Picault, appearing nauseous. "Have you looked up what those are for?"

"I did, Sir. Pentobarbital is part of the cocktail used to euthanize animals. The others are forms of anesthetics or tranquilizers, aside from amoxicillin which is an antibiotic... and"—Picault flipped through his notes—"Oxytocin, which is used to stimulate labour or lactation in animals."

After a brief pause, the detective chuckled. "I've heard of vet clinics having oxytocin stolen before because criminals often confuse it for OxyContin. Serves 'em right."

Picault snickered in response. "Maybe anyone desperate enough to take it will have enough drugs in their system, they can get high from breastfeeding off of each other."

Both men went silent, staring off into space before the detective blinked rapidly and shook his head. "You just pictured it too, didn't you?"

Picault shuddered. "Yep. Let's never mention this again. Ever."

"Deal."

By morning light, the entire crime scene had been processed and there was not a clue to be found beyond the list of what the thieves stole. Picault had been around long enough to know you couldn't assume who the guilty party was without evidence, but the complete lack of it suggested his initial guess was correct.

These men needed to be stopped, and there was only one more chance to make that happen. He was going to need a miracle.

Or a karmic intervention.

OBSTRUCTION OF JUSTICE

J ustin's phone rang, and he noticed Alvin's name with a photo of Fluffy lighting up his truck's Bluetooth-enabled screen. Justin had been enjoying his time with his new friend, and since the criminals hadn't struck for weeks, the Suburban Watchdogs were at a loss about how to track them down. They'd all been keeping an eye out but had seen no action since the encounter with Scarlett. As a result, Justin had more free time on his hands, so he'd spent the last couple of Thursday nights with Alvin at the clinic.

It was an average Thursday, and Karma was eager to see her friend.

"Hey, Alvin."

"Hi, buddy." His voice was groggy and gruff, with none of the usual enthusiasm Justin had grown accustomed to.

"What's wrong? You sound glum, chum."

"My clinic was robbed last night. Bastards stole half of my inventory, some of my prescription pads, and all of our cash."

Justin nearly veered his truck off the road but righted it before disaster struck. "Seriously? Did you call the police?"

"No, the police called me. I was there half the night. I was just calling to let you know I'd be closed today because I'll have to go in and get everything put back together, and I need some sleep. I've been up since two."

Disappointment flooded Justin's stomach, but he pushed it aside because there were bigger problems to address. "How 'bout you take a nap, and when I'm done for the day, Karma and I will stop by to help you get the place fixed up?"

"Nah, I couldn't ask you to do that. Not after you've been working all day."

"It's no trouble. I can even bring Ollie so he can watch the dogs."

Alvin was silent for a beat before he replied, "All right, then. But no hard feelings if you're too tired or something comes up and you can't make it. I'll manage just fine, but it would be nice to have some company. Those losers didn't just take dangerous drugs; they've made me not feel safe in my place of business now."

Fury overtook the disappointment Justin had been feeling. Alvin was a good man, trying to do good work, helping animals. He didn't deserve this. Neither did any of the other small business owners who had been victims of the tall man and his friends. Justin was determined; once he helped Alvin get his clinic put back together, he was calling a meeting of the Suburban Watchdogs so they could stop these guys once and for all.

After a full day at work, Justin returned home to change out of his work clothes, feed Karma, and pick up Ollie. Being home wasn't always peaceful if Scarlett was on the loose, but lately she'd seemed more docile. Justin was grateful for the unspoken truce they'd reached—though it was more of Scarlett committing to the silent treatment than a truce.

The two Peterson boys and their dog climbed into Justin's truck and headed for downtown, where Justin parked behind the vet clinic, unbeknownst to him, in the exact spot the criminals had the night before. He knocked at the back door, since it was locked, and waited for Alvin to let them in.

"Justin. Thanks for coming." The doctor reached his hand out to shake his friend's. "And you must be Ollie. I'm Alvin."

"It's nice to meet you, Sir." A young woman stepped out from a room into the hallway, and Ollie gasped. "Chloe?"

She turned toward the new arrivals and a smile appeared on her sweet face. The young girl had light blonde hair, much like Ollie's, and exposed her braces when she smiled. "Ollie? What are you doing here?"

"My dad asked me to come along to help clean up."

Alvin gestured for Ollie, Karma, and Justin to come inside, locking the door behind them.

"Fancy that. You kids know each other?" Justin asked.

Ollie replied, "We were in Mrs. Hanover's split class last year, so we have different teachers this year. She's Daisy's friend."

Karma and Fluffy were bouncing around each other, doing their traditional greeting, and seeing both his son and his dog so happy warmed Justin's heart, even under the circumstances. "Why don't you two take the dogs into the lobby and keep 'em busy while Alvin and I get some stuff done?"

"Okay, Dad." Ollie eagerly skipped forward, introducing himself to Fluffy and allowing her to sniff him. She was a much more gentle greeter than Karma, who looked proud to show off her small human to Fluffy.

The kids and dogs disappeared, leaving Alvin and Justin alone near the office door. "I tell you, Justin. These guys have aged me ten years. I couldn't sleep a wink today, as tired as I was, because I was terrified of what they're going to do with those drugs and prescription pads. That's like a free ticket to get whatever a pharmacy offers. I can't get it out of my head that I could be responsible for someone overdosing."

Justin placed a hand on his friend's shoulder. "Al, listen. None of this is your fault and you're not responsible for any of it. Those guys broke in and stole your drugs. They're the only ones to blame."

Alvin blinked away the water pooling in his eyes and gave Justin a nod. "I guess all I can do now is make sure it doesn't happen again. I need a new system to keep medications stored that won't allow for this sort of thing to happen."

Each moment since Alvin's phone call that morning seemed to have grown Justin's anger toward the elusive robbers. It was bad enough when they came into his town and started terrorizing a place that was generally peaceful. It was definitely bad enough when they showed up at his house and threatened him and his wife. But seeing firsthand how their actions had impacted his good friend, that was the icing on the cake. The cherry on top. The straw that broke the camel's back. Every tipping point cliché in existence.

"Don't worry. Their time as free men is short. I'm sure of it."

The two men worked in relative silence for the next hour, when Chloe yelled from the lobby, "Daddy! There's a police officer at the door."

"I'm coming. Don't answer it." Alvin asked the kids to take the dogs to his office so he could speak with the unexpected guest. The dogs dutifully followed their kids into Alvin's office, so once he heard the door click, he turned the locking mechanism on the front door and opened it wide. "Good evening, Constable Picault."

As Picault was about to explain to Dr. Harper the reason for his visit, he heard a familiar, yet unwelcome, voice. His entire body tensed, awaiting that devilish dog to pounce on him.

Justin rounded the corner, and Picault noticed he was alone. "Pee-cult. Long time, no see. How are you?"

Not long enough. "Mr. Peterson, what are you doing here, at another crime scene?"

Alvin glanced back and forth between the two men. "What's he talking about? *Another* crime scene? How do you know each other?"

"Uh... it just so happens that I saw the robbers fleeing the pharmacy a couple of months ago... Then I was out and about when they robbed the jewellery store, too."

"I was willing to accept that twice was coincidence, but finding an innocent man at three crime scenes seems to be unlikely, wouldn't you think?"

"Unlikely it might be, but that's the truth. Alvin and I are good friends, and he called this morning to tell me what happened. Ain't no mystery there."

Picault turned to Dr. Harper. "How long have you and this man been friends?" Even saying those words felt strange because Picault would be more inclined to schedule a colonoscopy for fun than spend time with Justin Peterson.

Alvin stammered, "A… a few weeks, I guess. We met last month at canine night."

"Canine night?"

"Yes. At a craft brewery in Newmarket. They host it once a month."

"I see. And did Mr. Peterson approach you? How did this friendship come about?" Picault was eyeing Justin, analyzing each adjustment in body language, but the man didn't seem uncomfortable.

"I… I guess I approached him. I was admiring his dog and saw that he was alone, so I sat down to talk to him. He… he has a friendly face."

Picault was satisfied the doctor was telling the truth, and it seemed unlikely that if Justin were casing the man, he wouldn't have made first contact. Still, it couldn't be overlooked. Not when they had so little to go on. As much as the short man didn't appear to be a criminal mastermind, he could be a skilled actor.

"So you struck up a conversation, and then what?"

"Uhh… we talked about dog breeds, and I told him I was a vet. Then he asked me about his dog's flatulence problem."

"Flatulence?"

Alvin nodded, and Justin's body language remained unchanged.

Picault pinched the bridge of his nose and took a deep inhale. "What next?" *I'm almost afraid to ask.*

"I told him to stop by my clinic one day the following week so I could give Karma some probiotics. He came that Thursday and it has been a weekly thing ever since."

"And has Mr. Peterson ever asked to see your stock room or about any of the drugs you have on hand?" Picault asked, confident he knew the answer. If he really wanted to interrogate Dr. Harper, he wouldn't do it in front of the person he was asking about. In this case, the real answers he needed were Mr. Peterson's reactions. It was fun to make him sweat a little. The shame was, he wasn't sweating at all. He stood off to the side, watching the interaction like any casual encounter.

"No… no sir. He's never asked or seen inside that room. Usually, he and Karma come through the back door, right into my office. We'll sometimes have a drink of scotch, shoot the breeze, then he goes home."

"Fair enough. It appears you just have a knack for showing up in the wake of our town's most notorious criminals, Mr. Peterson. Maybe you should consider forming your own faction of Neighbourhood Watch, then we could catch these guys." Picault chuckled, but for the first time, Justin's body tensed. *Interesting.* "Anyway, Dr. Harper, the reason I stopped by is to confirm that your security cameras were wiped, and we picked up nothing. There were a few prints collected, but we assume those were your employees or customers. My superiors asked me to stop in to see if you recall anything new since this morning. Any vehicles hanging around, or people walking by multiple times?"

The doctor shook his head. "I'm usually in the back, so I wouldn't have noticed. I mean, you're welcome to take the security tapes from the last month to see if anything catches a more discerning eye, but I'm afraid nothing caught my attention."

"Okay. If you don't mind, I'll take you up on that and gather the old footage while I'm here. Chances are the perpetrators covered their tracks, but we might get lucky."

Alvin turned to retrieve said security camera video from the hard drive in the utility room, leaving Picault and Justin alone in the lobby.

"I've never known someone to have such dumb luck in all my life, Mr. Peterson. All the police departments who have been searching for these guys haven't seen a trace of them, yet you keep showing up nearby." Picault wanted to press Justin while he was alone to see if he faltered at all.

Justin shrugged one shoulder and forced a laugh. "I'm not sure you know what luck is, Pee-cult, because it seems to me that would mean never having those bad guys in our town at all."

"You're right on that. I'm just confused about how you keep showing up at their targets."

His shifty eyes darted around the room and finally settled on a potted plant in the corner. "There's no easy answer to that. Beats me. If Karma hadn't farted in her yoga class, I never would have seen them the first time. Then I wouldn't have spotted them at the bookstore, and I wouldn't have thought they were trying to rob the bank."

"Exactly. Dumb luck." Picault rocked on his feet and hesitated to say his next words. "I heard about the men showing up at your house, Mr. Peterson. I'm relieved no harm came to you or your family." As much as he may not like the irritating man, Picault wouldn't wish any harm on him either.

"Karma handled them. They should know, Karma is a—"

"Here's the footage, Constable Picault. Is there anything else I can get for you?" Alvin returned to the lobby, glancing back and forth between the two men whose conversation he interrupted.

"That'll be all, gentlemen. I'll be back if there's anything else, but in the meantime, be diligent and keep your eyes open for anything suspicious. Take care."

Picault exited the office, breathing out a tension-filled breath, happy to put some distance between himself and Justin Peterson. The man was a gnat. Regardless, he and his renegade dog were the only reason any progress had been made in catching The Magic Men, so as much as he'd like to get out a flyswatter, he was willing to tolerate the annoyance a little longer. There was only one more chance to catch these guys. Failure was not an option.

BREACH OF TRUST

Picault had a much-deserved day off, but his mind was plagued with the events of the past few months. Alliston had never been a euphoric, crime-free haven, by any means, but people could walk through town after dark without being afraid. The Magic Men hadn't been overtly violent, but any animal has the capacity for violence when backed into a corner. Humans are the most vicious animals of all, and that potential for violence had everyone on edge. Beyond that, people of the town felt violated by the persistent break-ins, which had them distrusting the police.

˙   So, as much as Picault needed a day off, he wanted to unravel as much of the mystery surrounding The Magic Men as he could.

He started out on the south side of the main street, walking past *The Gadget Factory*. He considered the facts of that heist: During business hours, employees tied up, goods and cash stolen, alarm system present but not activated.

As Picault browsed the aisles, the two young men working paid no attention to him, continuing their animated conversation from behind the checkout counter. Perhaps they weren't fazed by the robbery, or they figured they didn't get paid enough to put themselves in harm's way. Nor should they have to. Ten minutes browsing the electronics store, Picault found nothing helpful, so he left.

Another hundred yards down the street, on the north side, was *GoldenWood Furniture*. They had taken an entire week to get their showroom cleaned up, and another three weeks beyond that to have everything restocked. While the thieves hadn't made out with much that would be of any use to them, they made life miserable for the business owners.

Picault stepped inside, noting the carefully curated furniture displays. He was a bachelor, and his furniture left a lot to be desired, so, for a moment, he considered purchasing a new sofa while he was there. He shook the thought from his head, determined to focus on what he came for. He considered the facts of the invasion: After business hours, no employees present, cash and personal information stolen, store vandalized, alarm system present but deactivated.

As he considered the crime, a woman, who looked to be in her early thirties, with long flaxen blonde hair and a soft figure, welcomed Picault, asking if he needed any assistance. He played along, wanting to get some insight into the store without seeming suspicious, and by the end, he bought a new charcoal grey sofa. The woman was effective at her job.

New sofa. No intel. Still, nothing of note.

His third stop was *LifeZest Pharmacy*, which was open for business the following day after the robbery but opened a few hours late. The door chimed when Picault walked inside, which it hadn't before. He figured that was their newest security measure. He spun his head around inside the entrance, looking to see if there were any other obvious security measures in place, and noticed a sticker on the window. The same company that provided security for *Hooves & Paws*. It would make sense that The Magic Men were able to determine which alarm system they'd be dealing with because every business they'd broken into had the company's logo on the window. Picault was sure of it.

Just to be thorough, he left the pharmacy, crossed back to the north side of the street, and walked by the jewellery store. Sure enough, there was the same sticker. He wandered down the street, trying to find any other businesses with the same security logo, but there were none. The only five on the street with that logo had already been hit.

Picault was irritated he hadn't made the connection sooner, because he may have been able to stop Dr. Harper's clinic from being robbed had he noticed.

That revelation gave Picault something new to go on. It may be a dead end, but at least it was something to investigate. He had been longing for a promotion for so long and wanted the higher-ups to see his potential. His motives for catching The Magic Men weren't selfish, though. He wanted to put an end to their crime spree. He just wouldn't complain if catching them resulted in his promotion, too.

Day off or not, he walked back to his SUV and drove to the station. He was going to relay what he'd found to the detectives.

Chen was on duty, sitting at his desk with paperwork edge to edge, and three takeout coffee cups littered across his workspace. "Picault, what are you doing here? In street clothes?"

Picault glanced down, taking in his navy polo shirt and jeans. "I was walking downtown, and I noticed something. I was hoping to run it by you."

"Give me a second." Chen scrambled to sort some of his paperwork, shoving things haphazardly into file folders and sweeping his empty cups into the garbage can he lifted from under his desk. "Sorry, I'm up to my eyeballs in Magic Men stuff, and nothing seems to be panning out. I hope you've got something good."

Picault relayed what he had discovered, and Chen was cautiously optimistic that it could turn into a decent lead. He told Picault he'd make some calls to the security company and let him know the outcome, but he didn't want to leave, knowing they could have a break in the case. Picault hung around listening to Chen speak to the security company representatives and get passed from one person to the next since no one seemed to have an answer.

When Chen ended the call, he blew out a breath and slumped in his chair. "They were reluctant to provide any information without a warrant, so I'm afraid I didn't get far. I told them they didn't need to give me specifics, but I wanted to know if the same technician installed the systems on each of the addresses."

Picault sat up straighter in his chair, eager for the answer.

"It was four different guys who installed them, and each one was done in a different year. The newest one is three years old, so I doubt our perps are employees."

That's not what Picault wanted to hear. Well, he was happy to hear that employees weren't responsible, but he didn't want to hear they didn't have any answers. "What else did they say?"

"Not much. They wouldn't give me addresses for other businesses in town with their systems. They're probably trying to save face now that it's obvious their systems have been targeted. They'll have to do damage control if that gets out. Business before safety." Chen rolled his eyes.

Picault was irritated. For a company that made money protecting people and places, they weren't putting their customers first by shutting out the police.

That was usually the way, though. So often the police would try to help and get caught up in so much red tape, they'd be mummified by it all.

His co-workers on duty might not be able to spend their shift cruising town looking for window stickers, but there was nothing to stop Picault from using his day off to discover potential targets.

So that's exactly what he did.

Armed with a list of businesses and an approximate date for their next strike, Picault was hopeful he'd finally have a win. A win for the town, and for his career.

DANGEROUS DRIVING

It had been two weeks since the robbery at Alvin's clinic, and no one had seen hide nor hair of the offenders since. At least, none of the Watchdogs. The criminals' ability to disappear like a thief in the night gave clarification as to how that term came about.

Morrie was working his typical shift after getting the kids off to school. Midway through the day, he opted to grab a bite to eat nearby, rather than go home for lunch like he normally would. He had spent the morning in Tottenham and had a few more jobs in the area that afternoon, so the twenty-minute drive each way made going back home an impractical choice for lunch.

He pulled into the *Tim Hortons* along the main street, wanting a hot coffee more than anything, despite the rising temperatures outside. Food was a secondary concern. He parked his work van beside a black Mercedes Sprinter van with solid panels in the back. As far as work vehicles went, that was top of the line and he was jealous of the lucky person whose work splurged for such a luxury. His decrepit twelve-year-old Ram cargo van left a lot to be desired, but at least it started each morning without fail.

About halfway to the door, a gigantic man walked out of the building carrying a tray with three drinks on top of a box of baked goods.

Morrie came to an abrupt stop as he stared at the pale man. He'd never seen someone so massive in person. It was as if Justin's childish drawing had sprung to life. There was no mistaking who the man was. Morrie blinked several times before pulling his phone from his pocket, earning him a glare from the big man, so he offered an awkward wave in response. When the giant continued past, Morrie took a few steps toward the coffee shop door, and snapped a photo of both man and machine, discovering the jumbo-sized man was climbing into the coveted Mercedes.

The vehicle's brake lights came on and they pulled out of their parking spot, onto the road heading north—toward Alliston.

Morrie opened the Suburban Watchdog group chat that Justin insisted on and sent the photo to his friends.

Whitey: *Looks like they're investing back into their business. Spotted just now in Tottenham with new wheels.*

Within minutes, all three men responded back with different reactions.

Scar: *Are you safe?*

Corky: *You didn't talk to them, did you?*

Fat Tony: *Are you following them? Let us know where they go and we can meet you there.*

After ordering his coffee and a toasted everything bagel with cream cheese, Morrie took a seat by the window overlooking the main street and pulled out his phone to reply.

Whitey: *I'm fine. No, I didn't talk to them and I'm not following them. I didn't have the chance, even if I wanted to.*

He unwrapped the paper surrounding his carb-heavy lunch, took a bite of his bagel as his phone started ringing. He chewed quickly, trying to swallow down his food to answer.

"Hello."

"Why didn't you follow them, man? That could have been the break we were looking for. Maybe they're casing a place in Tottenham and that's why we haven't seen them."

Morrie ripped off a small piece of his bagel, popping it in his mouth. He had a finite amount of time before his next appointment and couldn't waste it on this conversation. "They pulled out right after I pulled in, Justin. I didn't have a chance to jump back in my van and tail them. That would have been highly suspect if I did, anyway."

"You're right. Sorry, Whitey. I just really want to catch these guys after what they did to Alvin." He huffed a sigh. "At least we know what they're driving now. That's good work."

"That was the best I could do under the circumstances, but now we know what to watch out for." He stuffed another bite of food in his mouth, unconcerned about manners, when it came to Justin. "Listen, I have to hurry to eat and get to my next appointment. We can talk tonight, okay?"

"Sure thing, Whitey. See you tonight."

The excitement Justin was feeling having a break in their criminal hunt was palpable. Two weeks of searching, feeling like his countless hours driving around, being hot boxed by Karma's farts, were all for nothing. The information from Whitey was a step in the right direction.

Justin stared at the grainy zoomed-in photo on his phone, committing the license plate to memory and determined to keep his eyes open in search of another break.

He continued on the rest of his day, working quickly and efficiently, scouring every sideroad and driveway he passed for signs of the big black vehicle. All the time he'd been searching for a black pickup truck, which was an exercise in futility because black pickup trucks and farm country went together like alcohol and bad decisions. Having something different to look for was a relief. There weren't many Sprinters in the area.

Before he wasted more time searching for a vehicle that could be as easy to spot as a moving needle in a rolling barrel of hay, he made a stop at *The Gadget Factory*. There was something poetic about them possibly having a hand in the crew's undoing. Almost like... Karma.

Justin left the store with his purchase in hand, and after speaking with the employees, one of whom was tied up in the brazen robbery months prior, he could confidently say he was willing to do whatever it took to bring the bad guys to justice.

Thursday evening, Justin stopped in to see his friend Alvin at his clinic, which appeared to have recovered from their robbery, but Alvin was still on edge. His nervousness and anxiety surrounding the break-in added fuel to Justin's anger.

Karma and Fluffy danced around the small space in Alvin's office as he handed Justin a tumbler of scotch. He sat down behind his desk, releasing a tension-filled sigh. "Things don't feel the same in this place anymore. My staff are all scared, clients are afraid to come in here. We've lost so much business in the aftermath, even putting everything back together can't make us whole again."

Justin's hand clenched his glass. "I'm sorry, Al. You didn't deserve this. I swear on my daddy I'm going to catch these guys and make them pay for what they've done to you."

"Oh, now. None of that crazy talk. The police said they're taking care of it. We just have to trust that they will."

"I'm serious. My neighbours and I have been after these guys since they destroyed the furniture store. Karma even saved some jewellery from the robbery last month."

Alvin's mouth gaped open as he looked between Karma and Justin. "How did she manage that?"

The decision to confide in Alvin became easier, seeing how distraught he was over his business being targeted. Justin wanted to put his friend at ease. He relayed the events from the jewellery store robbery from his perspective and explained why he and Corky were there in the first place.

"So you've seen these guys who the police across the province haven't been able to catch?"

"Sure have. So has Scarlett. They came to our house."

Alvin spit out the drink he was about to swallow. "What?"

"It's a long story. Scarlett was jealous, kicked Karma out of the house, but she's a loyal girl, so she didn't leave. Crooks spotted her, tried to break into the house and she stopped them. Scarlett came out to see what the barking was about and saw the men."

The good doctor is speechless. "Wha... how... but..."

"Everything is fine. But I promise you, Al, I'm going to stop these scumbags if it's the last thing I do."

"Don't be going all *Ninja Turtles* on me now. The police have something to go on, and that's good work, but you can't put yourself in harm's way."

Justin's eyes lit up at the comparison, flattered to be spoken about in the same sentence as his childhood heroes, but his determination defied logic. Nothing anyone told him would lessen his desire to see those men behind bars. "Don't you worry your pudgy, shiny head, Al. I've got the best backup a guy could ask for."

Alvin's forehead developed twin creases between his brows as he looked at his tactless friend but said nothing.

"Well, I better get home. Ollie might need help with his homework."

Alvin snickered, but Justin didn't get the funny part.

"See ya next week, Al. Thanks for the drink. And don't worry about a thing; the Suburban Watchdogs are on the hunt." With that, Justin and Karma exited the office and left via the back door. They might not have had any new information, but Justin had a renewed fire in his gut, pushing him to put a stop to the crime spree. One way or another.

TRESPASSING

Justin spent eleven days straight being sent from one job to another, all over the county, which included Alliston and its vast surrounding area. The plus side was that he had been able to spend a lot of time with his number one girl, Karma, driving from one place to the next. After Scarlett's treatment of Karma in the past, Justin wasn't willing to leave his beloved dog home with her.

He had yet to try Alvin's advice about talking to his wife to see if there was anything he could do to fix things, but it was on his to-do list. After years of being yelled at, he was having a hard time pushing a talk with Scarlett to the top. Justin was contemplating what he could do to make his wife happier when something caught his eye. As he headed down one of the concession roads, running parallel to the nearest highway, he spotted a black Sprinter, just like the photo Morrie sent a week earlier.

After pulling over a hundred feet past the driveway, Justin turned to Karma. "This could be our break, girl. I'm going to get out to check the license plate."

Karma blinked a response, and he was regretting not putting more effort into learning Morse code. He blinked back in a random sequence, hoping it conveyed the appropriate message.

Once he had the package from the electronics store, he pulled out his phone, double-checked the license plate number in the photo, but was confident he had it memorized, and moved swiftly along the tree line toward the driveway's entrance. Peeking around the largest tree, he watched for several moments for any movement. He neither saw nor heard anything, so he moved forward, closer to the vehicle. He maintained cover behind a smaller tree, and again waited a few moments to ensure he was safe to make a mad dash for the vehicle.

With fluid movements, Justin darted across the driveway and dove behind the large van so anyone inside the small bungalow wouldn't be able to spot him. From that position, he equipped the vehicle with a GPS tracker. It may have been designed for nervous parents to keep track of their teenagers, but it could very well be the undoing of a prolific crew of wise guys.

He rushed back to his work truck, hopped in the driver's seat, short of breath from the mad dash. "I did it, Karm. We've got 'em now."

Justin pulled out his phone and texted his fellow Watchdogs in their group chat.

Fat Tony: *You'll never guess who I just found.*

Scar: *Jennifer Lopez?*

Corky: *Yao Ming? What is it with you and JLo?*

Scar: *She's an icon.*

Whitey: *What have you done?*

Justin was elated to tell his friends what he had accomplished. Aside from the birth of his son, he'd never been so excited in his life.

Fat Tony: *I planted a GPS tracker on their van. Battery only lasts 2 weeks, so it's now or never, Watchdogs.*

Whitey: *How did you get a GPS Tracker?*
Never mind. I don't want to know.

Before his good fortune ran out, Justin sped off toward home, adrenaline coursing through his veins. Things were finally coming together.

The entire evening after Justin returned home, he had the tracking app open, monitoring any movement. Scarlett complained about him finding his phone more interesting than her, and instead of replying with nonsense, he opted to follow Alvin's advice and communicate.

"Sweet Cheeks, I'm keeping an eye on the bad guys. I'm not trying to ignore you. I just want to keep you and Ollie safe."

Scarlett's face morphed into one reflecting sincerity and appreciation for the first time in years. "Really?"

"Of course. You might not like me anymore, but I'll always love you. I can't do anything else right, but I promise to do this." Justin's voice broke as he spoke, feeling the crushing disappointment of a failed marriage.

A tear slid down Scarlett's cheek as she dropped into the seat beside Justin on the sofa. "Justin, it's not that you can't do anything right. I see everything you do for us, and how much you love Ollie. I guess it just bothers me that you don't love me like that... and somewhere along the way, I think I stopped loving myself."

Justin's heart clenched at hearing his wife's honesty. "I'm sorry, Scarlett. I know this isn't the life you wanted for yourself—being married to a plumber."

"Your job has nothing to do with it. I don't even think *you* have anything to do with it. I'm just struggling to find my purpose. Ollie is at school all day. You're at work. All the other moms in the neighbourhood go off to work each day, and I don't think any of them even like me. Then you got Karma and stopped paying attention to me altogether. I know I didn't handle it well, but that day you chose her over me broke me."

The tears falling down his wife's cheeks hurt Justin's heart more than he could have imagined. All this time, he thought she hated him. Alvin was right. Communicating was important. "I'm sorry, Scarlett. We'd been arguing for so long, it never occurred to me that you'd want to go out with me. I'll make it up to you."

"Really?"

"Yeah. You can come to the next canine night at the brewery."

Scarlett scowled at her husband when his lips turned up in a mischievous smile and he cracked up laughing. For a moment, they laughed together, and it was the first peaceful moment they'd had for a long time—at least while both of them were awake.

Justin's phone beeped, indicating the criminals were on the move. He asked Scarlett to sit and watch their movements with him in a Watchdog-esque GPS tracker and chill at-home date.

The blue dot didn't travel far, and within ten minutes it was back in the driveway Justin knew they started from, so he wasn't concerned they were up to no good. He explained his plan for catching the bad guys as Scarlett expressed her desire to help. She was looking for something to give her purpose and helping her husband put past demons to rest seemed like a good place to start.

She understood better than anyone why it was so important for him to stop these guys.

STALKING

Scarlett was feeling better than she'd felt in years. The night before, she and Justin had a heart-to-heart and cleared up the misunderstandings that had been festering between them. Her life had a purpose beyond keeping the house clean and preparing meals again. Justin was trusting her to monitor the movements of the men who came to her home and scared her all those weeks ago.

Her husband made her agree not to follow the men anywhere, and if they came close to their house, call June for help, then the police. June made it no secret she still had a firearm in her home and wasn't afraid to use it. At ninety-two, a life sentence didn't seem like much of a deterrent.

Scarlett watched the blue dot move across the virtual map of their town, tracking the movements of the men and noting any stops they made. So far, they'd only been driving around in aimless circles with no pattern to their route. They hadn't stopped once, but Scarlett came to realize they had looped down Wellington Street three times.

The way the GPS tracker worked, the dot bounced across the screen in jerky movements as the signal refreshed every few seconds. It was hard to tell if the men slowed down at any spot in particular, and she wanted to know.

She grabbed her purse and keys, then threw on a pair of shoes to dash out the door.

Two doors down, she knocked. When the door crept open, Scarlett was staring at the one person she trusted to have her back, even if she smelled like Earl Grey tea and mothballs.

"Hi, June. Are you busy?"

The woman leaned on the door jamb with a sour expression on her face. Her usual. "I've been retired for thirty years. Trust me, I'm caught up on everything pressing."

"I... uh... well..."

"Spit it out. Just because I'm bored enough to knit myself some knickers doesn't mean I want to stand here all day."

"Right. Sorry. The men who came to our house are the same ones breaking into businesses in town. I know where they are and want to watch what they're doing, but Justin made me promise I wouldn't. I thought maybe you..."

"Say no more. Let me get my gun and my bulletproof vest."

Bulletproof vest? "Oh, I don't intend on getting near enough to them to..." Scarlett stopped speaking when she heard ammunition clicking into the chamber of a gun while June's head was tucked in her foyer closet. *Best not annoy her right now.*

June backed out of the closet and practically dragged her bulletproof vest to Scarlett, her old bones not strong enough to carry it. "This is for you. My shot isn't what it used to be."

Scarlett's eyes widened, regretting her decision to involve her neighbour. "Maybe we should just—"

"Lock 'n' load. Mount up, Crimson."

Crimson? This was a bad idea. "Sure. I'll just keep this in the van," she replied, patting the Kevlar vest. "I guess let's go?"

"It's about time this town saw some action. This must be the most boring place on Earth," June added, hobbling down the sidewalk with her curved back and bad hip toward Scarlett's minivan. "It's been years since I was part of a good old-fashioned drive by."

Scarlett tripped on air as she neared her vehicle, suddenly terrified of a granny with a gun. Her hands were shaking as she opened the door for June, and despite her suggestion, the elderly woman was not willing to part with her sidearm.

One last check of her phone showed the GPS tracker was looping around on the far side of town. That would give the ladies time to get themselves in place.

Scarlett pulled up behind four other vehicles parked on the side of the road and turned off her van. She yanked the handle to lean her seat back so she could stay hidden. It never occurred to her that June's cotton ball head would stand out so much against the green grass and brightly coloured gardens lining the street.

Afraid to ask the woman a simple question for fear of being shot, holding up a silk scarf, Scarlett quietly suggested, "June, do you want to wrap this around your hair? It's… it's beautiful, but…" The words died in Scarlett's throat as the black Sprinter van turned onto the street coming from the opposite direction.

She watched as the vehicle kept a steady pace, slowing ever so slightly in front of a home that doubled as a hairdresser. Confused, she kept watching from her spot, slouched in her seat. When she glanced back at June, the woman's head was tucked to her chin and she appeared to be asleep. *Oh, please don't be dead.*

Once the large van passed, Scarlett reached her hand out to feel for the woman's breath, not wanting to wake her, and removed the gun from June's grip. She wrapped it in her silk scarf, and secured it in her centre console.

A quick text to Justin let him know what she'd learned.

Sweet Cheeks: *They're looking for something on Wellington. Not the main street.*

Instead of texting, Justin called, and Scarlett jolted to answer before it woke June. "Hello," she whispered.

"Why are you whispering?"

"Um... I'm with June and she's having a nap."

"You called her over? Did they come near the house again?"

Scarlett didn't want to lie to her husband—especially when they'd just turned a corner by being open and honest—but she knew he wouldn't approve of what she was doing and didn't want to worry him. Even she wasn't sure it was a smart idea. "We were just hanging out. You know? Us girls." She let out a nervous giggle.

"Well, okay then. Not sure how you have a visit with someone who's taking a nap, but I'll let you get back to it. Good work watching the GPS. Love you."

Scarlett's heart warmed at hearing those words. It had been far too long since her husband said them, and even longer since she believed he meant them. "I love you too."

She went back to her surveillance duty, and when the criminals were a good distance away, she went around her van to lay back the passenger seat so June wouldn't wake with a sore neck. It also helped to keep her hair out of anyone's line of sight.

The sprinter van went past four more times in the next ninety minutes before it stopped for a brief second and one man she recognized jumped in the sliding door. They were on the move immediately, and according to the tracking app, headed back to where they started their day from.

Confident the men were far away, Scarlett turned on her van and pulled onto the street, slowing in front of where the man jumped in. A doctor's office. More specifically, the doctor's office Nicole Morris worked at.

That's their next target. If Scarlett had it her way, it would be their last.

It took some creative storytelling to explain to June why she was asleep in Scarlett's van upon returning home. Something about a mechanical bull and a skipping rope. Don't ask. She hobbled back into her house, without her firearm, mumbling something to herself.

When Justin came home for the day, shortly after Ollie had gotten home from school, Scarlett greeted him with an enthusiastic smile. They ate dinner as a family, including Karma, who had taken to sitting at the table with her big brother, and things were feeling peaceful in the Peterson house again.

Once Ollie finished his homework, bathed, and went to bed, Scarlett sat down to tell Justin the truth about what she had discovered—June's handgun and all.

He wasn't happy she had put herself at risk, but he was pleased with the results. He kissed her with renewed vigour and told her how grateful he was. To her surprise, not grateful for her information, but because she was safe.

Justin said he needed to report in with Morrie stat so he could be informed of the impending threat to Nicole's workplace. He sent Morrie a text to meet him outside to take Karma for a walk. It was urgent.

Morrie met Justin outside fifteen minutes later, and it only took a few words for them to morph into Fat Tony and Whitey.

"You're sure?" Whitey asked.

"Scarlett tracked the GPS today, and they circled the block seven times. On their final round, a guy came running out of Nicole's work. We're pretty sure that's their target."

Whitey felt sick to his stomach. All the times he wanted to give up to keep his family safe, he never could have predicted this being the result. He was tempted to tell Nicole to quit and never go back, just to keep her out of harm's way.

"It doesn't really make sense, though. What are they going to get from a doctor's office? They don't have much there for drugs or money. It seems like a wasted effort. Maybe they just had an appointment."

"Whitey, if they had an appointment, one guy would have driven himself. They were casing the joint. I know it. This is their next target."

With a sigh of resignation, Whitey braced himself for another crime, way too close to home. Again.

He returned inside, after they walked Karma a few kilometres, and explained to his wife the situation. Nicole, being the tough, determined woman she was, said she wouldn't leave her co-workers to fend for themselves. She'd go to work but keep her eyes open for anything suspicious.

Reluctantly, Morrie agreed, and he drifted into a fitful sleep.

Fat Tony and Karma arrived back home and filled Scarlett in on the conversation with Whitey. Scarlett was convinced the men were preparing to hit the doctor's office and was grateful Justin trusted her instincts. It was nice, feeling as though she had contributed something helpful.

An hour later, Scarlett fell asleep in Justin's arms with the dog at the foot of their bed. Even if she took up half of their sleeping area, Scarlett had warmed up to the slobbery beast. Maybe Karma wasn't all bad. You got what you gave with her.

BREAK AND ENTER

*T*onight is the night. The day had arrived. The culmination of Gord's entire criminal career. His swan song. After this, he and Earle could travel down to Mexico and live like kings until they were old and grey… rather… older, and greyer. Sleeping in until noon, drinking whenever, wherever, unlimited women. It all sounded too good to be true. But one more flawless heist, just like the last one, and his dream would become a reality.

"You guys got everything loaded in the van?" Gord asked his crewmates.

"Yep. Saddled up and ready to ride, good leader." Earle smirked at Gord and took an exaggerated bow.

"I've got everything," Nelson added from the hallway as he walked toward the eat-in kitchen. "I wiped everything down to get rid of our prints and burned all the bedding and stuff out back. Shouldn't be a trace of us to be found."

"Good man. Thanks for looking after that. After tonight, gentlemen, we'll be free to live the lives we've dreamed. It's been a pleasure working with you both."

"Ah, boss man's gone soft on us, Dunne," Earle jested.

"Screw off. Fine. I don't give a flying sheep's arse what happens to either of you, as long as I get my loot and get out. Every man for himself. That better?"

"Yeah. That's more on brand." Earle clapped Gord on the back. "We love you too, you big ogre."

Gord rolled his eyes. "Let's ride."

Being late Spring, the sun still hadn't fully set when all the businesses in the area closed for the night. Their last target was the one and only business they planned to hit that wasn't on the main drag. It was on a street running parallel, but more residential. For that reason, they needed to be extra careful, but if they played their cards right, they'd blend in easily. A van parked on a residential street wouldn't attract attention like it would on an abandoned commercial one, so it should work to the men's benefit. The major downfall was that the police had a satellite office only half a kilometre away. The good thing was that it was mostly for administrative purposes and wasn't staffed outside of business hours, but the main detachment wasn't too far away, either.

They couldn't afford for anything to go wrong. In the past seventy-nine robberies they'd done, only two have had any type of hiccup. Hopefully, the small man and his dog got the message to keep their noses out of business that didn't concern them.

The men parked the van along the curb in front of their target, accessible for an easy getaway. Gord, Nelson, and Earle all sat silently in the dim light of their van, mere shadows under the setting sun, waiting for all nearby houses to plunge into darkness. It took over an hour before the last TV shut off, and a shadow moved through the living room of the home across the street, signalling the neighbours had gone to sleep.

"Let's give them another thirty minutes, and if nothing else catches our attention, we move. Remember, no screw-ups this time," Gord instructed the other men.

Thirty minutes later, Earle said, "Time to move." He stepped out of the Sprinter and walked to the side entrance of the doctor's office, where he worked his magic, deactivating the alarm. A moment later, he gave Gord and Nelson the all-clear to join him.

The three men moved with haste through the office. Nelson came in days earlier pretending to be a patient looking for a new primary-care physician. The office had recently upgraded to a new charting system done on iPads, meaning what the bandits were really looking for was easy to grab.

This job wasn't about petty cash or narcotics. They were looking for personal information. Identities to steal and sell to the highest bidders. Medical reports were one of the easiest ways to do that. If they did the job right, this would be their most profitable heist, and would set them up for retirement as they had planned.

Gord was in one doctor's office, where he not only collected three tablets, he also found drug samples and prescription pads. He scanned the room, seeing if there was anything he missed, when he spotted a safe in the corner. No one kept a safe unless they wanted to protect something valuable. This wasn't something they picked up on in their recon, but Gord wasn't about to pass up the opportunity to crack a safe. For all he knew, it could have been his last high-stakes opportunity to do so.

The old-school dial was child's play, and when the locking mechanism clicked, Gord pulled the door open. Before he could take in the contents, an alarm sounded.

Loyalty may have earned Earle a spot on this crew, but his failure to do his job meant his usefulness had reached its limit.

"Earle, I swear, you're a useless idiot. Come on. The cops' ETA is only a couple of minutes."

"The alarm isn't even coming from here. It's coming from outside!" Earle shouted in defence of his skills.

Gord realized his friend was right. Something triggered an alarm in the daycare building next door. Talk about bad luck. Without another second's hesitation, he darted toward the front door, knowing he had unlocked it when he went past for this very reason. His crew followed.

The warm summer air barely had time to register on Gord's sensitive skin before he was lying in a heap at the bottom of the stairs with his friends moaning on his back. *What just happened? And why are these idiots moaning when I broke their fall?* Middle age and excessive height had not been kind to Gord's joints, but adrenaline helped to mask the pain he felt when he stood, coming face to face with the short man he'd been dreaming about putting down like a rabid dog.

The Watchdogs had been staring at the GPS tracker for days. With the help of Scarlett, they monitored the app twenty-four hours a day since her recon with June. They suspected things were going to go down soon, so when the crooks got in their vehicle and headed toward town, late in the evening, a flurry of text messages were sent, and the men were dressed and ready to roll out within minutes.

They parked Nicole Morris's SUV down the street from her workplace and jogged to get into their pre-determined positions—everyone except Brendon; he just walked quickly.

Corky, Scar, and Karma were patrolling the back side of the doctor's office, waiting for the right minute to call the police. They went radio silent with the other guys after reporting there was no movement at the rear. Whitey and Fat Tony were stationed at the two-corner, while Scar and Corky were to watch the four-corner. This was a tactical trick they learned from watching too many action movies. Starting with the northwest corner of a building, you label them one through four. By placing teams at opposite corners, all four sides of the building were covered, and no one was alone.

In theory, it worked perfectly fine, but nobody saw the men go inside. Apparently, determining their locations using compass directions caused some confusion for the Watchdogs. Instead of the four-corner, Corky and Scar set up position on the one-corner, leaving the three-four side of the building without eyes.

Brendon was questioning whether they had the right place and wondered if the criminals were hitting the business to the west of their location.

"I'm going to go check next door and make sure we're watching the right target. Stay here with Karma. I'll signal you if I find anything."

Corky offered a fist bump, acknowledging Scar's plan. "Be careful. I'll have your back from here."

As Scar approached the building next door, he didn't see any movement there either, and he was not sure why anyone would want to rob a daycare, anyway. What would they be looking for? Dirty tissues and pureed carrots? Toys with missing parts and foam nap mats? Didn't seem likely, but he continued his reconnaissance. Cupping his hands around his face, he peered in the back door, trying to glimpse something suspicious. Nothing. He pushed down on the handle of the glass door to see if it was unlocked, but instead of the door releasing open, an alarm started blaring. *Whoops.*

He bounded back over toward Corky and Karma, out of breath from the twenty-metre run. *I should have done more exercise than the diddly squats I've been doing for ten years. Monday. I'll start on Monday.*

"What happened?" Corky whisper-shouted from his position, crouched at the one-corner where Scar left him.

"I was checking if the door was open and set the alarm off. Any sign of them?"

"Nothing, but I heard a commotion up front."

Upon hearing those words, the two men snuck their way toward the two-corner, with Karma eagerly trying to get ahead of them, straining her leash.

They heard bickering between two men, one of whom sounded like Justin. "How did you get here? Did someone leave your cage open?"

The men glanced at each other, rolling their eyes. Before they approached any closer, Corky called 911. He whispered the situation to the operator, who assured him help was on the way. The police station was close, so all they had to do was stall to make sure the bad guys didn't get away.

When Scar peeked his head around the corner, he spun back around, grabbing Corky's arm and whispered, "They've all got guns pointed at Whitey and Fat Tony. Three of them. These are definitely the guys."

Fear gripped both Corky and Scar, but Karma was still itching to get in the mix of things. The men did the only thing they could think of and dropped the dog's leash, praying she wouldn't get herself shot. No one wanted to relive *Turner and Hooch*.

GRAND THEFT

F at Tony was trying to stall. He wasn't as stupid as everyone thought. Being underestimated had always been his greatest asset. He was known as the shrimp, the runt, the guy everyone overlooked. In order to survive, he needed people to sell him short so he could slide in under the radar. Sure, staring down the barrel of a gun was terrifying but being paralyzed by fear wouldn't improve the situation. The bear mace in his holster also wouldn't help because if he made a move for it, there was no guarantee he'd be fast enough to avoid getting shot. He had to appear unfazed by the threat and keep the men talking. He was confident the rest of the Watchdogs would have his back at the right time.

From the corner of his eye, he spotted his loyal friend creeping around the three-corner of the building. Stealth-mode activated, moving with a panther-like grace. He smiled to himself, and when he heard sirens in the distance, he knew he had to act or the men who had been terrifying the people of this great town for months would run.

"Chock-a-block!" Fat Tony shouted, staring at the Goliath wannabe who was about to meet his David.

The man-mountain's face twisted in confusion hearing the unusual word, but that was short-lived as a copper-coloured beast flew through the air with precision as if she was fired out of a skilled slingshot and locked her jaw on his gun-wielding arm. He pulled the trigger, but Karma's assault forced his arm to the right, so the bullet grazed past both Whitey and Fat Tony. Sirens grew louder and help was getting closer by the second. The big man was frantically trying to release the dog from his arm, but she was fierce and determined.

Three police cars came screeching to a halt on the road in front of the doctor's office, boxing in the Sprinter van parked at the curb.

An unfamiliar officer was the first to shout, "Nottawasaga OPP. Everyone put your hands up."

"Karma, release." Fat Tony placed his hands in the air but called off his dog, hopeful the police would stop any of the three outlaws from shooting him in the side of the head while he was turned away from them.

Karma returned to sit at her master's side, wagging her tail.

Whitey was standing beside Fat Tony, hands in the air, completely silent. Corky and Scar had moved around from the side of the building with their hands raised as well. The only ones not complying were the crooks caught red-handed. The three of them had their hands lowered at their sides, guns still in their grips.

"Drop your weapons and put your hands over your head. This is your final warning."

The police officers were staying back, shielded behind their open car doors and the crooks' vehicle, weapons drawn. As far as they knew, they'd arrived at an active shooting situation, and it wasn't obvious if anyone was on their side.

"These guys here have been runnin' amok in our town, making everyone scared. We caught them in the act, robbing this here doctor's office." Fat Tony didn't turn his head to look, but he could sense the tall man glaring at him. "Arrest them. We've got your backs."

A loud growl sounded from beside Fat Tony, and it wasn't Karma, but before the big man could do any harm, an officer fired a taser, dropping the man to his knees. Quickly, the police moved in, forcing the other two men to drop their guns, and the entire encounter was over.

With the big man laid out on the ground, Karma strolled over and slurped her tongue across the hulking man's face, leaving a thick layer of drool. "Get this thing off of me." He spit multiple times. "This is police brutality. Somebody stop this thing!"

He should have known you can't stop Karma.

When Picault pulled his patrol car to a stop in front of the medical clinic that he had noted in his potential targets list, he couldn't believe his eyes. He spotted Justin Peterson standing before a man who could be mistaken for a Nephilim, with no fear on his face whatsoever. His delinquent dog was dangling from the arm of the big man as he flailed about, and two other men watched on in horror with guns dropped to their sides. Mr. Peterson and three other men were dressed in black polo shirts and khaki pants like some kind of GAP-sponsored dad uniform.

The Sergeant first on the scene announced their arrival, which was a requirement when approaching an active crime scene—like the sirens, flashing lights, black and white cars, and uniforms didn't make it obvious—and the rest of them pulled out their weapons. Some officers opted for their firearm, but Picault and Billings took out their tasers, hoping to diffuse the standoff without deadly force.

The situation appeared to be reaching a boiling point, as they usually did with Justin Peterson involved. After giving his beast the command to release the tall man, Justin still couldn't resist running his mouth, forcing Picault to fire his taser at the man. A small part of him wouldn't mind seeing Justin get a little roughed up, but given the size difference, it wouldn't be a fair fight. Plus, Picault took an oath to uphold the law, so that would be immoral. Entertaining, but immoral.

After the three men in question were arrested, the other four were separated to be interviewed, and three out of four didn't cause an issue. The men followed their assigned officers to different spots in the general area and proceeded to explain their perception of events.

Once again, Picault drew the short straw and was forced to deal with the man who was as likeable as a thumb-tack-studded toilet seat. "Mr. Peterson. I warned you multiple times that if I found you around another crime scene, I was going to arrest you. Turn around and place your hands behind your back."

"Ah, come on, Pee-cult. We were trying to help. We knew you guys were strapped and overworked. We just wanted to stop these guys."

"Whatever your intentions were, you've gotten in the way more times than you realize, and I'm a man who keeps my word. Now, stop resisting and turn around."

Justin winked. "Well, shoot, Pee-cult. I could never resist you."

Justin's comments made patting him down more awkward than it should have been, but Picault found something he hadn't expected. "Mr. Peterson, are you wearing body armour?"

"Just a vest." He shrugged with his hands placed on the roof of the patrol car. "And the bear mace, there."

"Do I want to know where you got it?"

"Oh, *Canadian Tire*. The vest is June's."

"And June is…"

"My neighbour. Her husband was an RCMP Sergeant Major. She left her gun in my wife's van too, but I never touched it."

It took a moment for Picault to digest that information. First order of business was to get Justin out of the way. Picault secured handcuffs around Justin's wrists and placed him in the back of his patrol car. He had no intention of taking the man to the station or pressing any kind of charges, but after all the times the man had been an intense irritation, this was the easiest way to keep him out of trouble for a while.

Once Mr. Peterson was handled, Picault walked toward the curb where three angry-looking men were seated. Detective Staff Sergeant Chen was asking questions, trying to get one of them to break, but naturally, when they were together, no one would snitch. Questioning them together could sometimes breed a false sense of security.

"So, which one of you fine citizens dropped the cell phone for us to obtain our intel?" Picault stood over the seated men with his thumbs hooked in his pockets.

The smallest of the three men cowered.

The big man's face turned red at an alarming speed, and he lurched his body toward the smaller man. "Dunne, you idiot. Is that why you changed your number? You didn't think to tell us? I knew you couldn't have had a psycho ex girlfriend."

Constable Dunham separated the men, who both had their hands restrained behind their backs, so at best they'd knock each other out with head butts.

"Gee, I wonder why, Gordo!" Dunne shouted in reply once he was moved a few feet to the left. "You're so understanding and level-headed. I should have just come clean. You would have understood, right?" He huffed out a mocking laugh and turned away from the gloomy red giant.

Their unified front is cracking. Excellent.

"Both of you, shut up. They're trying to turn us against each other. Keep your wits about you and don't say another word." The crazy-haired man, who looked the least intelligent of the group, was the first one to say something smart.

Once those words were spoken, neither of the other two would say anything else, so the next step was individual interrogation. Chances were, one of them would cave when they got back to the station, where the real questioning would begin. They were caught red-handed with stolen goods and illegal firearms, which they discharged in a residential neighbourhood. No judge in their right mind would let them loose for a long while.

Karma had finally caught up with them.

CITIZEN'S ARREST

The next ninety minutes were spent combing the scene, interviewing Mr. Peterson's friends, and taking copious amounts of notes. No T's uncrossed. This case needed to be a slam dunk. The Magic Men had been handed to the OPP on a silver platter, so they couldn't slip up.

The tallest of Mr. Peterson's friends seemed to be the most articulate in his replaying of events. As stupid as Picault thought their actions were, he had to commend their bravery. Vigilantes weren't something he wanted to encourage, but in this case, public intervention helped get these criminals off the streets. He wouldn't tell them that, though.

After Billings finished his interview with Mr. Morris, Picault opened the back door of his patrol car to find a scene he hadn't expected. Justin was snoring, laid out across the back seat.

"Mr. Peterson." He waited a few seconds. "Mr. Peterson!"

The irritating man jolted awake, popping himself upright, which was impressive considering his hands were secured behind his back.

"Mr. Peterson. Could you step out of the vehicle, please?"

"Oh, yep. Sure thing." He turned his head, wiping his mouth on the shoulder of his black polo shirt, then placed both feet on the ground and hoisted his small frame to stand.

The three other men came running over, along with the furry beast who allegedly saved the day. "Justin, are you all right, man?" Mr. Morris asked.

"Yeah, Whitey. I'm good."

Picault mouthed to himself, 'Whitey?'

"So, Picault, what charges am I up against? And you can forget about reading me my rights. I'm married... I know how important the right to remain silent is."

The officer's head jerked back in surprise. "You said my name right."

Justin snickered. "I'm not an idiot. I knew how to say it right after the first time you told me, but I thought a nickname would be fun."

"You thought Pee-cult was a good nickname for an officer of the law?"

"Nicknames are not his greatest talent," the Spanish man added.

"Shut up, Scar. I'm great at nicknames. Tell me Whitey Bulger, Scarface, and Corky Romano aren't three of the greatest mobsters of all time." Justin scowled at his friend. "And I recognize a man who takes life too seriously when I see one."

"Scar, Whitey, Pee-cult... and you are?" Picault asked the brunette man whose colour was only just returning to his face.

He breathed an exasperated sigh. "Corky."

Picault could no longer help himself and burst out laughing. It was the first good laugh he'd had in the months of chasing the criminals, making him and his fellow officers look like incompetent morons. "What are you guys? Some sort of small-town dad gang?"

"Suburban Watchdogs, I'll have you know. And without us, those guys over there would have gotten away again. So, you can arrest me if you want, Pee-cult, but I have no regrets." Justin's voice was loud and confident before it morphed into a near whisper. "Just Remember what I said about my bowels. I'll need an alternative arrangement to prison."

The four men all stared down at the spitfire of a man in front of them.

Unfortunately, I remember, Picault thought. "I might not have appreciated your methods, Mr. Peterson, but I can't argue with the results. Thank you for your help in apprehending these men." Picault reached for his key ring and turned Justin to face the vehicle so he could unlock his cuffs. "I'll need you to stick around to answer some questions, but you're not under arrest."

"Thanks, man. Call me Fat Tony."

Picault howled with laughter once again until he saw the straight face of Mr. Peterson staring back at him. "Fat Tony. Sure."

There was just one thing that had been nagging Picault since the jewellery store robbery, and since the situation was all but resolved, he needed to know. "Say, Fat Tony, how come you were so determined to catch these guys? Most people just turn the other cheek and leave us to do our job."

Justin's eyes flicked around from one person to the next until his gaze was directed upward with water pooling in his eyes. "When my ma was pregnant with me, her and my daddy had to run some errands. One stop was the bank because this was before debit cards and ATMs." He blinked several times, which made a single tear run down his cheek and Picault found himself choked up by the emotion on the man's face. "Dad ran into the bank while Ma waited in the car. Just then, three armed men walked in to rob the place. Ma was terrified, but because she was pregnant with me, she ducked down to hide in the car so she wouldn't be spotted. Then she heard gunshots."

The four men stared at Justin with their mouths agape.

"Your dad?" Picault asked.

"Apparently, he tried to stop them, so they shot him to set an example for the rest of the people in the bank. They used him like a pawn, and there was nothing anyone could do. But because of him, everyone else got out safely."

Picault's voice was sombre as he responded, "I'm so sorry, Justin... er... Fat Tony." Suddenly the man's motivation to stop his town from being terrorized made perfect sense. He might not be the smartest guy around, but you couldn't discount his bravery and integrity. "Your dad would be proud of you."

Justin nodded and issued Picault a meek smile. "When my momma told me what happened—why I never got to know my dad—I promised myself if there was ever a time for me to stop someone from getting hurt, I'd do whatever it took. That I'd be brave like my dad, no matter what."

The three other men, who were presumably members of the Suburban Watchdogs, gathered Justin into a group hug. The dog, who had been sitting loyally at her owner's feet, jumped up to join in, nearly bowling them all over, but they included her in their embrace.

"You want in on this, Pee-cult?" A voice shouted from inside the huddle.

"Nah, I'm good, Fat Tony. Thanks."

The men broke apart and Picault excused himself to tend to other duties for a few minutes, but before he could walk away, Corky said, "If you ever find yourself free on a Friday night, you're welcome to join us at our headquarters anytime."

The other three men nodded in agreement, and warmth swelled in Picault's chest, feeling appreciated by members of the community. *Maybe these guys aren't so bad after all.* "I'll see what I can do." He walked off with a smile on his face to wrap up the best night of his policing career to date.

He learned an important lesson. Everyone had a story. Everyone had faced some sort of tragedy in their lives. What they chose to do about it was the difference between The Magic Men and Suburban Watchdogs.

ELDER ABUSE

Nelson Dunne may have lived his life as a thief, but the code most career criminals lived by didn't apply to him. He wasn't part of some deep-rooted, widespread mafia who would come after him for ratting on his friends. He wasn't full-blooded Italian, and no one was tracking his family back to the old country. He was accountable to no one. In his mind, he had nothing to lose, and everything to gain.

The moment the interview room door latched shut, he began negotiating. By detailing every heist that Gord, Earle, and himself had been part of over the last six years, he worked his sentence down to two years of probation. Gord and Earle were already going down, with or without his help, so Nelson gave himself permission to take the easy road. The police had nothing to close the cases in the previous twelve towns their crew had terrorized before they mistakenly walked into Alliston. The allure of "solving" those crimes was too much for the crown attorney to pass up, so Nelson helped them pad their stats.

Spreadsheets, detailed heist plans, and bank statements helped to make Nelson's case and provided a slam dunk for the prosecutors.

His plans of retirement would have to wait, as he was forced to get a real job and prove to his probation officer that he was no longer a menace to society, but you know what they say? You can't teach an old dog new tricks. And as much as he wanted to ride off in the metaphorical sunset, there was an old dog he had a score to settle with.

Every August, the town of Alliston, known as the potato capital of Ontario, hosted a three-day long potato festival to celebrate their most prolific crop. Friday evening was always marked with a parade marching through town—specifically downtown, right past the businesses that were impacted by the crime spree earlier in the year.

As a special thank you, Alvin purchased a "float" in the parade which he planned to use to advertise his veterinary clinic, but it had a much more important purpose. His daughter Chloe helped him decorate the float, which was essentially a flatbed trailer pulled by a pickup truck. After some handiwork and creativity, the father-daughter pair stepped back to look at their finished product and couldn't help but smile.

"It's perfect." Alvin dusted off his hands, which were still sticky from the excessive amount of hot glue and duct tape used to create their masterpiece. "Thanks for your help, baby girl. Now we just need to get our guests of honour on board."

The night of the parade, half of the town showed up to line the streets. The Watchdogs and their families were gearing up to walk the two kilometres to the edge of the parade route for their annual tradition. This year, as they were waiting outside of their houses for Brendon to finish loading his bag with snacks, a parade float pulled up in front of Justin's house and honked its horn.

When Morrie, Josh, Justin, and their families looked up at the monstrosity, they all beamed with excitement.

Justin poked his head in the truck's cab and spotted his good friend, Dr. Alvin Harper. "What's up, Doc?"

"Thought you guys might need a lift. Hop on!"

The parade float looked incredible, with a massive papier mâché French mastiff head with streamer drool hanging out both sides. It must have been four feet wide. A white picket fence surrounded the entire trailer, which made it safe and look more "suburban". The best part of all, aside from the mural of the criminals sitting in a jail cell, was the giant banner saying, "Thank you, Suburban Watchdogs."

Brendon came running out of his house carrying a backpack full of who-knows-what and halted when he spotted the creation occupying space in front of his house. "This is amazing!"

Even June hobbled down the sidewalk to see what the ruckus was about. If the Suburban Watchdogs were to give honourable mentions, June would be top of the list. Even though she fell asleep, her and Scarlett's intel was the final nail in the Magic Men's coffin. Though the neighbourhood was safer now that June's gun was no longer in her possession.

"What have we got here?" the old lady asked the group of kids gathered around the float.

"Dr. Harper made a parade float for our dads." Ollie beamed with pride at his father, standing on the float's platform. As scared as he was of June, he couldn't neglect his manners. "Would you like to join us, Mrs. Garin?"

For what may be the first time since her husband died twenty years earlier, June smiled. "That would be lovely. Thank you, young man."

The four members of the Watchdogs assisted June onto the float and got her settled, so she was safe and had a good view.

By this point, any neighbours who had yet to leave for the parade were outside watching the commotion. The smiles on everyone's faces couldn't be missed as all eight children, one elderly woman, four men, one beast, and three wives, stood atop the remarkable display. Karma had taken up her rightful place at the front, mimicking her likeness in papier mâché form.

Justin walked to the edge of the float and reached a hand out to his wife. "What do you say, Sweet Cheeks? Can I bring my leading lady? None of this would have been possible without you."

Scarlett eagerly jumped on board with a wide smile, and without hesitation, kissed her husband.

The whole experience of chasing criminals put things in perspective for the Petersons. After discussing with the guys what happened to his father, they helped Justin see that life was short, and it was important to cherish those who were important. Scarlett and Justin still had a lot of reconciliation ahead of them, but for the first time in years, they were both willing to try.

"I'm proud of you." Scarlett said to Justin as she gave Karma a pat on her massive head.

Justin returned her smile. He knew his parents would have been proud of him, too. His mom had passed away a few years earlier, but he'd vowed to never stop trying to make up for the ultimate sacrifice his father had made.

The next two hours flew by in a blur of cheering residents, smiles, and autographs. June had a nap. The children tossed candy at spectators. The wives soaked everything in, appreciating their husbands, children, and neighbours. The men were able to hop on and off the float throughout the parade route, and even Karma met and greeted a few adoring fans. Her drool was readily distributed to anyone who came within an arm's length; not one person complained. She had reached the type of celebrity status where bodily fluids of any sort were seen as some kind of blessing.

Once the parade was over, a local reporter asked to photograph the Watchdogs, including Karma, in front of the parade float for an article in the paper. With no new threats on the horizon, the Suburban Watchdogs soaked in the praise and cheers of everyone around.

At least, they thought all threats had passed. But while they were busy having their photo taken, Nelson Dunne made his way to the edge of the crowd near the men's wives and children. Knowing the dog was busy having her wrinkly face photographed gave Nelson the confidence to strike while he had the opportunity.

The sly man walked up behind a short blond kid, who was standing away from the other children, staring at his father with an irritating smile. Nelson's blood boiled over the attention the four loser fathers were getting. He finally understood Gord's blinding rage, causing him to reach out and grab the boy's black polo shirt.

The boy swivelled his head, and asked politely, "Please don't touch my Watchdog uniform, Sir." Once he finished speaking, fear flashed in his eyes, but before he could shout, Nelson clapped a hand over his mouth. Amongst all the clamouring of the crowd, no one would hear a brief tussle with a skinny kid.

Nelson stepped backward to pull the boy away from the safety of his friends and family but dropped like a sack of Allistonian potatoes. He hit the dirt, and before he could understand what happened, he was being beaten with something hard, but it wasn't doing any damage. Beyond that, there was screaming and cries for police from others around him. He knew he had to make a break for it.

The old lady they'd spotted mowing her lawn months earlier was whacking Nelson with her cane. Nelson would have laughed at her efforts, but she shouted, "Scarlett, get my Glock from my handbag."

Nelson knew he had to get away, or this deranged granny would shoot him. He pulled himself up onto his elbow, using his other arm to swat away the old batty, but didn't make it to his feet.

The monster dog that had tackled him at the jewellery store was on top of him again—this time, she wasn't in a friendly mood. Her jaws were clamped around Nelson's throat as he stayed perfectly still with his eyes wide. He knew one wrong move, and he'd be dog chow.

The entire confrontation occurred in less than forty seconds. One minute, the townspeople were watching their local heroes have their photos taken, the next, their local villain had his plan foiled once more.

Nelson knew his opportunity had passed. In a split second, the dog could rip out his jugular and he'd be a goner for real. He didn't even have the chance to shove her off and make a mad dash. She just would have caught up with him again. He resigned himself to the fact that he was busted and cursed his stupidity for not taking off to Mexico.

"Over here, Sergeant Pee-cult. This guy tried to grab Ollie. He's one of the baddens."

Even with jaws of death gripping his throat, it didn't stop Nelson from scowling at the short man.

"Karma, release."

The dog relaxed her hold on Nelson but didn't move from her position overtop of him until a familiar man with dark blond hair stepped up beside them.

"Thanks, girl." He reached down to pat the dog's head. "Mr. Dunne, I can't say I'm surprised to see you again, but I hoped I wouldn't." He grabbed Nelson's light blue button-up and forced him to stand. "You couldn't take your second chance and leave well enough alone, could you?"

Nelson sighed, not needing the cop to preach to him about his bad choices.

PROBATION VIOLATION

Picault tightened the zip cuffs around Nelson Dunne's wrists, smiling to himself. The decision to let the man off with two years of probation had irked Picault, and he had a feeling the lifelong criminal wouldn't be able to keep his nose clean for long. He was just happy he'd been able to watch him get taken down by a granny and a dog. That would do wonders for his prison rep.

Nelson was escorted off by Constable Leicester, who was working the festival grounds, along with Picault's new girlfriend Constable Denise Michaels. Picault gave his girlfriend a wink as she rushed off to tend to the job at hand. Everyone present relayed their take on events, and eventually returned to the festivities.

"That was a pretty fierce takedown, Mrs. Garin," Picault addressed June, who was seated on a bench at the edge of the fairgrounds.

Scarlett was seated beside her with red-rimmed eyes, holding the old lady's handbag. "She saved my son. Are these men going to keep being a problem for us, René?"

"Well, who knows what excuses they could come up with, but that man is on probation, so hopefully they throw the book at him."

"Thanks for having Karma's back, Pee-cult." Justin joined the small group, clapping René on the back.

"Anytime, Fat Tony." Picault smirked because that nickname still cracked him up after two months of regular use.

"We might have to make you an honorary member of the Suburban Watchdogs."

"I thought you guys were giving up your crime-fighting ways. Retiring from vigilantism."

"Well, that was the plan, but not if criminals think they can walk into our town without a fight." Justin puffed out his chest, as he was accustomed to doing when Fat Tony joined the chat. His Italian accent and hand gestures added to his big-man persona.

"We agreed you'd leave the crime-fighting to the professionals. I'm sure Scarlett and Ollie would appreciate it if you didn't stare down the barrel of any more guns."

Scarlett nodded, and June smirked.

"Speaking of, Mrs. Garin, did I hear correctly that you're carrying a concealed weapon?"

June looked up at the young Sergeant. "Now, Sonny, why would you think that?"

"Someone said you shouted for Scarlett to get your Glock."

"Who's the rat?" June scanned her surroundings, staring down anyone she viewed as suspicious. "I said 'get my clock.' You know, so we could time how long the coppers took to show up." The old lady set her face in a hard stare, and the intensity had Picault nervous. He'd stared down plenty of hardened criminals before, but not one of them was as tough as Mrs. Garin.

"Well, we should get June home, Pee-cult. We've all had a long day. We'll see you at Corky's place next Friday?"

"Wouldn't miss it." Picault said goodbye to his group of unlikely friends, including Alvin Harper, who had also joined in on the weekly guys' nights in lieu of his brewery visits. The six men, on paper, had little in common, but they considered each other a misfit family.

The best friendships could come from the most unlikely places.

Gord hadn't pictured retirement this way. Locked up in a maximum-security prison in Penetanguishene, separated from his one childhood friend, like a schnook. His lawyer couldn't even tell him where Earle was serving his sentence, but it wasn't like being prison pen pals was all that appealing, anyway.

He plunked down a tray of colourless, foul-smelling food on the table as he slid his hulking frame onto the bench. Luckily for him, his size and temper kept anyone from messing with him, but that didn't mean he was enjoying himself. Maybe a little trouble would make the place more interesting. He gagged down his disgusting lunch, not questioning what he was eating, as he'd become accustomed, and returned to his open cell without a word to anyone. Even his cellmate hadn't spoken to him and wouldn't if he knew what was good for him.

Later that afternoon, the literature cart came squeaking down the alleyway, and Gord opted for the newspaper. He'd never been one for reading, but he liked the newspaper and at least some kind of connection to the outside world. Maybe there'd be a nice lady in the classifieds he could send a letter to. If someone was willing to put their information in the paper seeking a life partner, their standards couldn't be too high. Some notorious criminals had fan clubs. He considered that for a moment until he remembered the stupid name the police had given them—The Magic Men. He'd have preferred something like The League of Extraordinary Wise Guys.

When Gord signed for his newspaper to accept the charges from his commissary account, he grabbed his reading material and climbed onto his bunk, which was about eight inches too short. Pulling the newspaper open, he let out a scream that even the prisoners on the other side of his cellblock heard.

"That damn dog!"

Yeah. Karma is a... female dog.

THE END

Thank you for reading Suburban Watchdogs. If you enjoyed the book, please consider visiting www.goodreads.com and/or the website you purchased the book from and leaving a review. Book reviews are a great help for authors to reach new readers. More importantly, we love to know what our readers think!

Find me online at linktr.ee/TiffanyAndrea

ACKNOWLEDGEMENTS

Thank you to my fantastic beta readers and cheerleaders, Lucia, Harriet, and Tara. I wouldn't have gotten this book over the line without you. I appreciated the feedback and constant reassurance from each of you.

Of course, I have to thank my two daughters, husband, and our goofy dogs for putting up with my unrelenting book-centric conversations and providing endless comedic inspiration. Your support means the world to me.

And, lastly, thank you to the members of law enforcement who genuinely put their lives on the line each day. May you never run into a real life Fat Tony.

(And on that note, citizens, please do not take it upon yourself to confront dangerous criminals. Remember what Picault said, it's their job to catch the criminals, it's your job not to be one.)

Also By This Author:

You Are Enough Series:
We're All a Little Broken: Book 1
We're All a Little Overwhelmed: Book 1.5
We're All a Little Guarded: Book 2
We're All a Little Tired: Book 2.5
We're All a Little Scared: Book 3

This women's fiction series focuses on various aspects of mental health and overcoming trauma. It addresses anxiety, depression, panic disorders, miscarriage, adoption, grief and loss, racism, discrimination, and more, but in a light hearted way that will also make you laugh. The entire series is set in Muskoka/Bracebridge, Ontario.

A New Leash on Life Series:
Total Bull (Angel and Damian)
Ay Chihuahua (Dina and Holden)
Tell-Tail Sign (Sophie and Boyd)
This series will consist of twenty interconnected standalone romantic comedies. Some characters from Suburban Watchdogs and the You Are Enough series will have cameos or their own starring role!
Sign up for my newsletter or follow me on social media to learn more.
Linktr.ee/TiffanyAndrea

Made in the USA
Middletown, DE
27 February 2023

25787066R00139